"Why [barcode] *to Marr*

Something in Shane's voice warned her against telling him the truth. She knew he would send her away if she told him that she loved him. Shane didn't want love; all he wanted was passion—and a son.

"I'm not sure, Shane." Her voice was brittle. "Maybe I like the idea of lifelong financial security."

She felt him stiffen and saw the anger in his eyes. "So, my little child-woman is mercenary after all. Well, if you want to sell yourself to me I don't see why I shouldn't take advantage of it. Certainly I'll marry you, Karen—for a while."

PHYLLIS HALLDORSON
like all her heroines, is as in love with her husband today as on the day they met. It is because she has known so much love in her own life that her characters seem to come alive as they, too, discover the joys of romance.

Dear Reader:
Silhouette Romances is an exciting new publishing venture. We will be presenting the very finest writers of contemporary romantic fiction as well as outstanding new talent in this field. It is our hope that our stories, our heroes and our heroines will give you, the reader, all you want from romantic fiction.

Also, *you* play an important part in our future plans for Silhouette Romances. We welcome any suggestions or comments on our books and I invite you to write to us at the address below.

So, enjoy this book and all the wonderful romances from Silhouette. They're for *you!*

Karen Solem
Editor-in-Chief
Silhouette Books
P.O. Box 769
New York, N.Y. 10019

PHYLLIS HALLDORSON
Temporary Bride

Silhouette *Romance*

Published by Silhouette Books New York

SILHOUETTE BOOKS, a Simon & Schuster Division of
GULF & WESTERN CORPORATION
1230 Avenue of the Americas, New York, N.Y. 10020

ISBN: 0-671-57031-5

First Silhouette printing September, 1980

10 9 8 7 6 5 4 3 2 1

Temporary Bride

Chapter One

Karen's stomach churned as she sat in the plush outer office thumbing through a copy of a slick picture magazine while waiting to be called into the inner sanctum by the sleek, efficient receptionist. Three girls had already been ushered in ahead of her and she was afraid that if she had to wait much longer she'd be sick. The suspense was made even more unbearable by the fact that she didn't have the slightest idea who was behind that office door or what he wanted from the woman he selected. She had answered a blind ad in the newspaper:

> Woman wanted. Age 21–30. No family ties. Must be free to relocate. No skills necessary.

The only address had been a box number.

Karen knew it was dangerous to answer an ad like that, but she was desperate. It had taken all her parents' savings and much more to pay the astronomical medical expenses before her mother died of a lingering illness. Then, just a year later, after her father had finally paid off all personal debts, he collapsed one morning and died of a heart attack, leaving Karen, at eighteen, with a heavily mortgaged house and not even enough money for the next payment. She'd taken college prep courses in high school that had left her eminently qualified for the college of her choice but untrained in any skill necessary to support herself. She had no close relatives and her pride would not allow her to confide her poverty to family friends, all college instructors like her parents.

Karen had seen the ad in a San Francisco paper and, after long deliberation, had answered it. The problem was her age. The ad said twenty-one and she was only eighteen. It had been easy to lie on paper but now she was to be interviewed in person. She wasn't sure they'd believe she was eighteen, much less twenty-one. She stood four feet eleven inches and weighed ninety pounds on her heavier days. Most of her clothes were bought in the children's department and she usually looked about fourteen.

Another girl came out of the office and this time the receptionist called, "Karen Muir."

The knot in Karen's stomach tightened as she stood and walked across the room on the three-inch cork platform shoes she had been lucky enough to find at a sample shoe sale. She had pulled her long chestnut hair into a chignon at the nape of her neck and worn the dark, simply cut dress she had chosen for her father's funeral. She crossed her fingers and murmured a silent prayer as she stepped into the private office.

The blond young man behind the desk stood as the receptionist introduced Karen and said, "I'm Mark Jefferson, Miss Muir. Won't you sit down?" He indicated a chair.

Karen was aware of his blue eyes discreetly taking in every detail of her small but compact body as she settled herself. The palms of her hands were sweaty and she clutched them together as she sat back and crossed her shapely legs in what she hoped was a nonchalant gesture.

The office was small but luxuriously furnished and had a spectacular view of the bay. She breathed a little easier. If this company, whatever it was, operated from this office, it must be solvent, at least. Hopefully it was also respectable. Mark Jefferson was smiling at her and his voice was friendly as he said, "I see by your application that you are twenty-one, but you've listed no previous work experience. What have you been doing since you graduated from high school, Miss Muir?"

She took a deep breath and plunged into the story she had rehearsed. "My—my father died very recently, but until then I was his research assistant. He was writing a textbook."

Actually it was true. She *had* helped her father with research for his book, but she'd also been going to high school at the time.

"And your mother?" Mark prodded.

Karen lowered her eyes. "Mother died a year ago. I was an only child, so now I'm all alone. I'm free to travel, if that's what you want."

He nodded. "May I ask if your parents left you well fixed financially?"

She didn't really see why that was any of his business, but maybe it would help if he knew she needed the job. She shook her head and there was a catch in her voice as she answered. "No. My mother was in and out of the hospital for years before she died and Dad had to borrow heavily. It was probably the strain of trying to pay back the debts that brought on his fatal heart attack. I was left with nothing and I need this job desperately."

She hated to beg, but she was terrified of what would happen to her if she had to compete in the job market with no training and no experience.

He wrote something on a pad of paper, then stood and said, "Thank you for coming, Miss Muir. You'll hear from us before the end of the week."

So Karen headed her compact car away from the congested streets of San Francisco to the small city in the valley that ran between the majestic Sierra Nevada mountains on the east and the Coast mountain range on the west and settled down to wait. By Friday she was a bundle of nerves and could no longer stand the four walls that closed her in as she paced around the house waiting for the postman to come or the phone to ring. She had to get outside, and besides, there was plenty to be done in the spacious flower gardens that had been her father's pride and joy.

She pulled on her blue jeans and striped pullover shirt, parted her gently curling hair down the middle and tied it back on either side with lengths of scarlet yarn, then resurrected an old pair of tennis shoes already stained with mud. The July sun shone relentlessly on the valley and as Karen crouched down weeding the garden, her face grew shiny with perspiration.

By noon the muscles in her back, shoulders, and legs ached and she was aware of a tormenting thirst. She finished with the bed of petunias and stood, wiping her hands on her already dirty jeans, and walked across the patio into the house through the sliding glass doors. As she stepped into the living room she heard the doorbell. With an impatient gesture she hurried to the front door and opened it.

The man standing there was a stranger—she was sure of that. She could never have forgotten him if she'd ever met him before! He looked to be in his early thirties—not exactly handsome, but his features blended well together and were framed by jet black hair. There were lines of tension around his firm mouth and the square cut of his jaw indicated a stubborn insistence on getting what he wanted. He towered above Karen. The brown business suit he was wearing was expertly tailored to fit across his wide shoulders and tapered to his slim waist and hips. The legs of his trousers molded around powerful thighs and Karen swallowed as she looked quickly back up to his face. His deep brown eyes held little warmth, although he smiled as he said, "Is this the Muir home?"

She nodded, quite unable to find her voice. She noticed another man coming up the walk as the first one continued. "Is your sister, Karen, at home?"

Karen blinked and answered, "I'm Karen Muir."

The first man stared and the second man, who by now was standing behind the first, gasped, "Karen!"

She recognized Mark Jefferson, the man who had interviewed her for the job! Oh, no! He'd caught her looking like a twelve-year-old tomboy who had been playing in the dirt!

She murmured an embarrassed greeting and invited the two men inside. The stranger looked grim as he snapped at Mark, "Is this your idea of a joke?"

Mark cringed. "So help me, Shane, she said she was twenty-one and she looked a lot different the other day."

The man called Shane turned to her. "Just how old are you, young lady?"

She shrank from the fury of his gaze as she stammered, "Eight-eighteen."

His eyes traveled up and down her tiny length as he snorted. "I don't believe you. If you're a day over fifteen I'll be surprised. Why on earth did you answer that ad? And where are your parents? I intend to see that they give you the paddling you so richly deserve!"

Karen had been taken by surprise and the guilty knowledge of her deception had allowed her to be intimidated, but now a slow anger was creeping through her and she pulled herself up to her full four feet, eleven inches as she glared back.

"Now just a minute! I don't know you and I've only met Mr. Jefferson once. What gives you the right to come to my home uninvited and unexpected and make threats? I can prove I'm eighteen years old and that my parents are dead. The only thing I lied about was my age, and I'm sorry about that, but it doesn't give you the right—"

She was working up a good head of steam when Mark cut in. "Hey, knock it off, both of you! Can't we talk about this in a reasonably businesslike way? Karen, this is Shane McKittrick, the man you would be—uh—working for. You're right, we had no business coming here without calling first, but Shane wanted to see you in the natural setting of your own home."

"It's a good thing I did, too," Shane snarled angrily. "Otherwise this blockhead might have made the mistake of hiring you." They were standing in the entrance way and he looked at Mark as he turned toward the door. "Come on, it's a long drive back to San Francisco."

Mark reached out and grabbed Shane by the arm. "Calm down, will you! I told you, Karen is the only one who met all your qualifications. I'm sorry she's younger than we thought but does age really make so much difference?"

"I might have considered a twenty-year-old," Shane grated, "but this one is nothing but a baby herself! You know as well as I do that she's impossible!"

Karen felt like a slave being auctioned off on the block. Besides, her throat was so parched it felt like sandpaper, and she'd lost her chance at the job—whatever it was—anyway, so there was no reason to be polite. She spoke bluntly. "Will you two either come in and sit down or leave? I'm tired, thirsty, and hungry, and I resent being talked about as if I weren't even here."

She turned and walked into the living room and the men followed, silent for the first time since they arrived. She gestured toward the couch in an invitation to sit and busied herself in the kitchen, washing her hands and fixing three tall glasses of iced tea. She carried them in on a tray and offered a glass to each man, then took her own and sat on a straight-backed chair, mindful of her dirt-caked jeans. The long, icy drink relieved the dryness in her throat and she watched out of the corner of her eye as Shane

McKittrick sipped his. She giggled at his look of surprise and said, "If you were expecting whiskey, Mr. McKittrick, I'm afraid it's way beyond my budget. I really meant it when I said I needed that job. If I'm lucky I'll get enough from the sale of the house to get by until I can take some training and learn to support myself."

Shane frowned. "You're selling this house? Why?"

She took another drink of the tea. "Because I can't make payments on it."

Shane glanced around the comfortable room then back to Karen. "Surely there must be someone to look after you."

Karen bristled. "I don't need anyone to look after me. All I need is a job."

Shane put down his glass. "You'll never find a job. There are child labor laws in this country. Run along and clean yourself up and we'll take you out to lunch."

Resentment burned through her as she stood. "I don't need to be fed like a disadvantaged child. I'm sure you are anxious to get back to the city, so—"

Shane looked at his watch as he cut in. "I'll give you five minutes to get under the shower. If I don't hear water running by that time I'll come and bathe you myself."

Karen gasped. "You wouldn't dare!"

He raised an eyebrow. "Would you like to try me?"

Twenty minutes later she was scrubbed and dressed in a cotton print sundress with a fitted bodice, spaghetti straps, and a full skirt. On a larger girl it would have looked fashionably adult but as Karen applied jade eye shadow to highlight her sparkling green eyes she realized that it made her look even more like a little girl. Oh, well, it didn't matter anymore. She might as well be comfortable.

Mark Jefferson was talking on the telephone when Karen came back into the living room. Shane McKittrick looked at her and grinned. "We've been looking up restaurants in the phone book and decided on The Copper Lantern. Mark's phoning for reservations."

Karen's eyes widened. "But that's the most expensive place in town!"

Shane stood and slipped his hand under her elbow. "I think between Mark and me we can manage to pay the bill."

The Copper Lantern was new and as elegant as Karen had been led to believe with its dark paneled walls, copper accessories, and Early American furniture. She fully enjoyed the rich ham and split pea soup served with thick slices of warm homemade bread and creamery butter. During the meal Mark and Shane, with their gently prodding questions, managed to learn most of Karen's history.

As she dug into a bowl of blueberry pie swimming in pure cream Mark grimaced and said, "How do you manage to eat like that and stay so petite?"

She grinned. "Richard used to say I'd pay for it when I get older."

"Who's Richard?" Shane asked quickly.

"He's a boy I used to go out with. He was a little chubby and claimed he could put on five pounds just watching me eat."

Mark chuckled but Shane apparently didn't see the humor. He frowned. "Are there any other men in your life?"

She paused, taken aback by his abruptness. "No, there aren't. I've been too busy the past two years for much social life. First Mother was so ill, and then when she died I spent all my spare time doing research for Dad's book."

Shane persisted. "And the book—has it been published? Do you get royalties?"

Karen shook her head and lowered her brimming eyes. "No. It was only about half finished when he died. I suppose once I start to work I'll have to pay back the advance the publisher sent him."

Shane and Mark glanced at each other and Shane spoke. "Karen, I can't use you in the position you applied for, it's impossible, but I have a large personal library in my home that needs sorting and cataloguing. It should take about a month and it will be at least that long before your house is sold. I can show you quickly what needs to be done and you'd live at my home on the Monterey Peninsula and receive a salary besides room and board. Are you interested?"

Karen looked at him with amazement. "You mean you're offering me a job after all?"

He nodded. "Only a temporary one, but it will tide you over until you sell your house and decide what school you want to enroll in."

She was still unsure. "But if I stay at your house won't your wife object?"

"I don't have a wife, but before you get any funny ideas, I'm usually only there on weekends and it's a big house with a housekeeper, cook, and several maids, not to mention the gardener.

I promise you we'll be properly chaperoned." His eyes twinkled and she knew he was making fun of her.

She toyed with her coffee cup. The offer was almost too good to be true. It took time to sell a house and get it through escrow, but her home had increased in value over the years, as had all real estate in California. She should have several thousand dollars left after the mortgage was paid off that she could live on and use to pay her tuition to a secretarial school until she was qualified for a job. She looked from Mark to Shane, who were sipping their drinks in apparent unconcern over whether she accepted the offer or not. Well, it might not make any difference to Mr. Shane McKittrick, but it was of vital importance to her. She had to start earning some money. She looked at Shane and managed a lopsided smile.

"Thank you, Mr. McKittrick. I can start anytime you'd like."

Shane stubbed out his cigarette in the crystal ash tray and stood. "Good. How about this afternoon?"

It had been a hectic few hours, but by late afternoon Karen was sitting between Shane, who was driving, and Mark in the front seat of the long, luxurious Lincoln Continental as it sped down the highway. She was beginning to have second thoughts. Whatever had possessed her to agree to pack up and leave her home on the spur of the moment with two men she knew nothing about? They seemed to be wealthy businessmen, but it could be a clever front. Nobody even knew where she was going—there hadn't been time to make phone calls. Shane, as he insisted she call him, told her she could write or make phone calls from his home, but how did she know where he was taking her, or why? She moved restlessly against the soft cream velvet upholstery and made an effort to understand what the two men were talking about. They paid no attention to her as they spoke of accounts and shipments and stock manipulations. Shane was obviously the head man, but she gathered Mark was an assistant or something equally close.

Boredom plus the smooth hum of the engine and the slight sway of the car combined to relax her so completely that she could hardly keep her eyes open. The day had been long and she had worked hard, first in the garden, then packing and getting ready to leave. She yawned and her head nodded as Mark's arm encircled her shoulders and made her comfortable against his broad chest. She slept.

It was dark when she opened her eyes and realized that the car was no longer moving but the chest against which she was sleeping was.

"Karen, wake up. We're here."

It was Mark, and he had an arm around her, holding her as he spoke. She jerked to a sitting position and blinked. "Where are we? How long have I been asleep?"

"Do you make a habit of curling up and sleeping in the arms of every man you meet?" It was Shane, on the other side of her, and he sounded irritated.

She was still half asleep and disoriented. "No. I-I'm sorry. I didn't mean—"

Mark got out of the car and reached a hand in to her. "Don't pay any attention to Grumpy there, Snow White. He's just put out because it wasn't his arms you were sleeping in."

Mark grinned and Karen slid out and had barely closed the door when Shane gunned the motor and drove on down the sloping driveway.

Even though it was dark, the house and grounds were well lit and she could see that the place was immense. It seemed to be built on the side of a cliff and she could hear water lapping against the rocks below.

The intricately carved oak door was opened by a tall, angular woman, fiftyish, with heavy dark hair brushed back from her face and worn low on her nape in a chignon. Her face was expressionless but her gray eyes fastened on their subject with chilling intensity. She greeted Mark with cool politeness and he introduced her to Karen as Mrs. Whitney, the housekeeper. Mrs. Whitney glided stiffly ahead of them down the mosaic tiled corridor to a spacious room at the back of the house. Karen gasped in awe. The sapphire blue carpeting felt ankle deep and the closed wall-to-wall draperies on two sides of the room were a complementary but lighter shade of azure blue and breathtakingly beautiful. The grand piano in the corner left plenty of room for several furniture groupings, and the paintings on the undraped ice blue walls were originals and expensive.

Mark was talking to Mrs. Whitney and Karen was just standing there trying to adjust to the magnificence of the room, when Shane came up behind them. He greeted Mrs. Whitney and said, "This is Karen Muir. As I told you on the phone, she'll be here for a month or so cataloguing the library. Please show her to her room and I'll have her bags brought up later." He turned to Karen. "Dinner will be served in half an hour. Don't bother to change."

His abrupt dismissal left Karen no choice but to follow the housekeeper's stiff back through a maze of rooms and hallways and finally down a flight of stairs. Mrs. Whitney explained coldly, "This is the lower level; it contains the main kitchen, laundry room, and the servants' quarters."

She made a right turn and led Karen into a wing consisting of a sitting room, dining room, and several bedrooms and baths. Karen's room was about like her room at home, small but comfortable. The furnishings were adequate, the closet was large, and she shared a bath with the room next door.

Mrs. Whitney stood in the doorway and her crisp voice was disapproving as she said, "Apparently Mr. McKittrick expects you to dine with him and Mr. Jefferson this evening, but in the future you will take all your meals down here with the rest of the employees. I hope you will not make a nuisance of yourself with Mr. McKittrick." She turned and marched off before Karen could say anything.

Dinner was served in a formal dining room that could easily seat fifty people. Karen was impressed and made no attempt to hide it as Shane seated her at the solid mahogany table covered with handmade lace and set with china, crystal, and sterling silver. As in the living room, two of the walls were draped but on the wall opposite her she recognized an original still life in oils by Paul Cézanne, one of her favorite Impressionists. Forgetting her manners, she slid off her chair and went to stand in front of it, giving in to the impulse to reach out and touch the canvas that had felt the hand of the master painter.

Behind her, Shane's voice was soft. "You like Cézanne?"

"Oh, yes—he tempered his flights of fantasy with realism—but I also like Degas and Monet."

"You'd like this clam chowder, too, if you'd sit down long enough to taste it," Shane teased.

Karen felt the warm color rush to her cheeks as she realized how rude she'd been to leave the table. "Oh, I'm sorry! I guess I got carried away."

She returned to the table and Shane stood and seated her again. "You seem to know a great deal about French Impressionists."

Karen nodded. "Yes—my mother taught art appreciation."

Mark spoke. "Was your mother an artist?"

Karen swallowed a spoonful of the clam-filled chowder. "She painted a little, but I'm afraid her talents lay in teaching rather than doing." She sighed. "Mother would have loved this house, too."

Shane looked at her thoughtfully. "Are you pleased with your room?"

Karen finished her soup just as Mrs. Whitney came with the salads. "Yes, thank you, it's very comfortable."

Shane looked a little disappointed and she wondered if he'd expected her to be impressed with the room. It was nice but certainly not impressive.

The salad was followed by a beef dish with vegetables and then freshly made ice cream covered with warm cherry sauce. Karen ate everything that was set in front of her but refused the seconds that Shane, with an amused expression, urged her to accept. When Mrs. Whitney began clearing the table Shane rose and said, "We'll have coffee in the den, Mrs. Whitney."

Mrs. Whitney nodded and murmured, "Yes, sir," but her eyes sought Karen's and the message in them was clear. *Don't make a nuisance of yourself*, they warned her again.

Karen would have liked to have had coffee in the den with Shane and Mark, but she had been reminded of her place in this household. She was an employee, not a guest, and it was time she remembered it.

She stood, too, but backed away as Shane started toward her and said, "Uh—I think I'd better go to my room and unpack."

Shane took her arm. "Taffy will unpack for you."

She looked at him. "Taffy?"

"One of the maids." He urged her forward. "It's probably already been done—now come along."

She sidestepped carefully, not wanting to seem rude but anxious not to upset Mrs. Whitney. "I'd—I'd really rather do it myself. I'll be ready to start work tomorrow. That is, if you'll be here to show me the library and what you want done."

He frowned impatiently and dropped his hand. "As you wish. I expect to be here all weekend so we'll have plenty of time to discuss it. Good night." He turned and walked out of the room and she knew she had displeased him.

The next morning Karen woke early and made her way to the large main kitchen on the other side of the lower level. She was greeted by a tall, slender man of indeterminate age dressed all in white. A big smile lit his face and he spoke with a heavy French accent. *"Bon jour, mademoiselle.* You are the new, how you say, librarian?"

She laughed. "Well, not exactly. I'm going to catalog the library. My name is Karen Muir."

He nodded his understanding. "Ah, then you will need breakfast. Sit down, sit down." He waved at the breakfast bar with several high stools and she slid into one as he poured her a cup of coffee. "I am Henri. You like your eggs scrambled, yes?"

Before she could agree, a high-pitched feminine voice, like the tinkle of a bell, sounded from the doorway behind her.

"Henri, love, could I have a three-minute egg in two minutes? I overslept yesterday and the Dragon has been breathing fire and smoke down my neck ever since. If I don't start cleaning Mr. McKittrick's room the minute he leaves it, she'll probably hang me by my thumbs." She spotted Karen sitting at the bar and squeezed onto the stool beside her. "Hi, you must be the new gal who shares my bathroom. Do you always shower at five-thirty in the morning?"

Karen smiled. "Sorry. I tried to be quiet. I'm Karen Muir."

The young face surrounded by blond curls dimpled in a grin and the hazel eyes teased as the girl said, "Apology noted and accepted. I'm Taffy Harris."

So this was the "Taffy" Shane had mentioned last night. She looked to be about Karen's age and was soft and curvy and purred like a kitten—the kind of girl men liked to gather up and take home.

Henri brought the girls eggs with side dishes of bacon and hot buttered biscuits. Taffy picked up her fork and said, "Thanks, Henri. I hope Mr. McKittrick doesn't decide to get up early." She turned to Karen. "Have you clashed with the Dragon yet?"

Karen blinked. "The Dragon?"

"Mrs. Whitney. You sure don't get a chance to fluff off around here. She's right there with her whip and chair. You're not really a member of the staff, though. I'm surprised you were put down here—I'd think you'd rate an upstairs room."

Karen shrugged. "Apparently not—this is where Mrs. Whitney brought me."

Taffy finished eating and jumped up. "Sorry, I gotta run. Don't let Mrs. W. browbeat you."

Karen followed a few minutes later, intending to try to find the library. She was anxious to examine the books she would be working with. As she passed the dining room she saw Shane at the table having breakfast. He glanced up and called to her.

"Karen! You're up early. Where are you going? Come sit down and I'll ring for your breakfast."

She stood there puzzled. "Oh, no, thank you, I've already had breakfast."

He frowned. "When?"

"A little while ago," she replied vaguely.

He motioned her into the room. "How did you manage to wander around without me hearing you? Sit with me and have some coffee, at least."

She sat down and took the cup of coffee he handed her as she wondered how he could have expected to hear her when there were two stories between them. She stirred her coffee and glanced around the room, then gasped at the panoramic view before her. The wall-to-wall draperies had been pulled open and the two outside walls were simply two huge windows with a breathtaking view of the Pacific. With a little cry, she jumped up and went across the room to gaze at the magnificent view.

She had been right last night; the house was built on the side of a cliff with the rocky coast below. Shane came up beside her and said, "Do you like it?"

She drew in her breath. "Like it! I've never seen anything so beautiful! Where on earth are we?"

He laughed. "We're on Seventeen Mile Drive, between Pacific Grove and Carmel on the Monterey Peninsula. Surely you've been here before."

She couldn't take her eyes from the cloudless sky and the smooth, shimmering ocean. "I've driven through after paying the four-dollar entrance fee, but I never dreamed that someday I'd stay in one of these houses. To think you actually live here! I don't see how you can stand to leave it."

He was standing so close that his shirtsleeve brushed against her bare arm. "I don't remember ever being especially impressed with either the house or the view. I was born here and never knew anything else. When my parents were alive it was a place to come back to from boarding schools, but now I use it mostly for business reasons. It's an excellent place to entertain, but I spend most of my time at my condominium in San Francisco."

There was a touch of sadness in his voice. She felt a twinge of sympathy for the little boy who spent most of his childhood away from home in boarding schools and said, "You must have been a lonely child."

He looked at her with a quizzical expression in his dark eyes. "Why on earth would you think that?"

She realized she'd overstepped the bounds of propriety and felt a surge of embarrassment as she hurried to apologize. "I'm sorry, I didn't mean—"

He held up a hand to silence her and his voice was low. "Don't be sorry—you're right. I'm just wondering how you knew."

She looked back at the peaceful scene on the other side of the glass. "When I was growing up my parents and I were never separated. It would have broken my heart if they had sent me away to school or left me behind when they went on vacation, but I'm sure the thought never occurred to them."

"You miss them very much, don't you." It was a statement not a question.

She nodded, not trusting herself to speak.

Shane's nearness and the tenderness in his voice were having a disturbing effect on her. He was a stranger. She should never have come here with him and yet she had no fear. She trusted him instinctively, knew somehow that he wouldn't hurt her. He could be gentle one moment and flare into anger the next, and yet she felt protected here in his home.

But was there another side to him? Why had he put that strange ad in the newspaper? What was the position that she was too young to fill? Why all the secrecy? If it was all honest and aboveboard, why didn't he hire a girl from an employment agency? Who was this man and what did he want?

Chapter Two

Karen ran her fingers reverently over the book before she replaced it gently in the glass case and locked the door. The library was half the size of the living room but the walls were lined with hundreds of books. Some were custom bound in leather, others encased in publishers' jackets, and then there were the first editions— worn, stained, and priceless. These were the ones that were kept locked behind glass.

Karen sighed and dropped wearily down beside Shane on the red velour couch in front of the brick fireplace. He looked up from the ledger he was working on and asked, "Are you tired?" He glanced at his watch and exclaimed, "Good heavens, you're probably starved, too—it's after one o'clock!" He closed the ledger and stood, reaching for her hand. "Come on—we'll go find Mark and have some lunch."

Mark had joined Karen and Shane briefly at breakfast, but they hadn't seen him since they left him to come to the library. It was a delightfully intimate room, and the hours had flown by as Shane familiarized her with the books and showed her how he wanted them sorted and catalogued. It would be a big job, one that would keep her working happily for weeks.

She put her hand in Shane's and let him pull her to her feet as he said, "I'll find Mark. You go freshen up and we'll meet you in the dining room in fifteen minutes."

She hesitated. "Oh, but I—"

Why did he keep inviting her to eat with him when Mrs. Whitney had made it plain that she was expected to take her meals with the rest of the staff in the kitchen? He was probably only being polite but it was awkward all the way around. She took a deep breath and continued, "You and Mark go ahead with lunch. I'll grab a sandwich and take it to my room. I still have some settling in to do."

Shane glared at her. "Damn it, Karen, what's the matter with you?" He seemed prepared to say more but controlled himself with an effort and muttered, "Oh, well, have it your way. Run along—I won't need you anymore today." He turned on his heel and stalked out of the room.

Karen had lunch in the kitchen on the lower level with Taffy and the two other girls on the housekeeping staff, Jolene and Erma. Taffy grumbled good-naturedly about the tyrant, Mrs. Whitney, and the other girls merely listened, neither agreeing nor disagreeing. When Karen could get a word in edgewise, she asked the question that had been bothering her.

"Taffy, I've never been in a house where the kitchen was in the basement. Isn't it awfully inconvenient running up and down stairs with the food?"

All three girls laughed so uproariously that Karen suspected her question had been a stupid one. Taffy, still giggling, explained.

"We don't run up and down stairs, silly—we use the dumbwaiters. Come on, I'll show you."

She led Karen to the wall and showed her the small elevators that conveyed the food and dishes from the main kitchen to the small kitchen next to the dining room directly above.

"And, love, this is not a basement." Taffy giggled again. "We are also on the ground floor down here. The house is built on a cliff and you just walk down the steps of the terraced gardens to get from one level to the other."

She led Karen into the sitting room and for the first time Karen saw the sliding glass doors that took up most of one wall and led to the rolling green lawn outside. Drapes had been pulled across the doors last night and this morning when she had gone through, but now Karen saw that the view of the ocean was almost as spectacular from here as from the main floor.

Taffy continued. "There's also a door in the kitchen and the help is expected to use it instead of the front door upstairs. I don't know whether that includes you or not."

"It most certainly does." There was no mistaking Mrs. Whitney's voice even before the girls turned to face her. She stood straight, unbending in both posture and attitude as her voice dripped disapproval. "Karen is an employee here and as such is subject to the same rules as the rest of you. Now, Taffy, I suggest you get back to the kitchen and help Erma clean up the dishes. I'm sure Karen has work to do also."

She turned and walked away, leaving the girls in no doubt that they had been reprimanded.

Karen was in the library scrutinizing the bookshelves and making notes of titles and authors when the door opened and Mark came in. He sounded relieved.

"Hi, there. I've been looking for you. We missed you at lunch but I don't blame you for not joining us. Shane was in a foul mood—hardly said two words and rushed off somewhere as soon as we'd finished eating."

She was surprised. Shane had been happy and in good spirits all morning. She couldn't imagine what had happened to upset him, unless it had been her refusal to have lunch with him and Mark. She instantly dismissed that thought as silly and returned Mark's greeting. They talked about her work for a few minutes until he changed the subject.

"Look, it's Saturday and you've worked all morning. Why don't you take off and come with me? We'll go for a ride. How about Fisherman's Wharf at Monterey? Ever been there?"

Karen was tempted; why not? Shane had told her he wouldn't need her anymore today. She agreed, and a few minutes later they were heading north on Seventeen Mile Drive in a brilliant yellow Corvette that Mark had requisitioned from the four-car garage. The drive along the bluffs was a stunning visual experience, and Karen insisted that they stop to examine the famous Lone Cypress, a stunted tree that had been tortured by the continuous winds into a grotesque shape but clung tenaciously to nearly bare rock on the cliff. A little further on they explored Cypress Point Lookout, where the sunny blue skies made it possible to see Point Sur and Point Sur Lighthouse twenty miles to the south.

At Pacific Grove they turned east off Seventeen Mile Drive onto Lighthouse Avenue and followed it to Fisherman's Wharf in Monterey. At the entrance an organ grinder ground out carousel music while his small gray monkey, dressed in a blue vest and hat, danced. Enchanted, Karen knelt and held a quarter in her outstretched hand. The monkey took it from her and kissed her on the cheek. His rough little tongue licked her smooth skin. It cost Mark five quarters before he could entice her away with the promise of a fresh shrimp cocktail.

The pungent odor of kelp and sea life assailed Karen's nostrils as they strolled past the open-air fish markets and poked around the jumble of tiny shops that offered gaudy souveniers, postcards, and imported gifts to gullible tourists.

They finished the day at historic Cannery Row, where the large warehouses had been converted into museums, art galleries, and antique and specialty shops. Dinner in the nautical atmosphere of the Lobster Grotto was a gourmet delight enhanced by a window in the floor and the view of the splashing waves below.

It was after midnight when they entered the driveway of the McKittrick estate. The grounds were well lighted and, while Mark put the Corvette in the garage, Karen started across the thick carpet of grass toward the kitchen.

"Hey, where are you going?" Mark caught up with her and took her arm, swinging her around. "You have to go up the steps through the gardens to get to the main door."

"But I'm supposed to use the kitchen door," Karen explained.

"The kitchen door!" Mark exclaimed. "Why?"

She shrugged. "I'm an employee, Mark, not a

guest, and employees are expected to use the kitchen door."

He stared at her. "What's this nonsense you're spouting?" His mouth opened, then closed, and his eyes narrowed as he scrutinized her face. "Karen, where is your bedroom?"

"It's down here in the servants' quarters." She saw the rage kindling in his eyes and said, "It's really very comfortable. I share a bathroom with Taffy."

He was angry. "And I suppose you're taking your meals in the kitchen, too. Is that why you haven't been eating with Shane and me?"

Karen nodded as Mark's hand dug into her arm.

"Well, I'll be damned!" He spat the words. "I understood you were in the room across from Shane's suite on the second floor. I wondered why I never saw or heard you in the halls up there." He shook his head in disbelief. "I thought he'd escaped the 'big boss' complex."

He took Karen's hand and started walking up the terrace steps. When she protested, he spoke grimly. "Look, honey, when you're out with me I'll bring you home through the front door. If Mr. "Big Man" McKittrick doesn't like it he can complain to me!"

Karen knew it was useless to argue and hoped everyone was in bed.

The entryway was in semidarkness, the only illumination coming from a low-wattage electric sconce on the wall. Mark closed the door and started to lead her toward the living room but she hung back.

"No, Mark, it's late and I'd better go to my room. I shudder to think what Mrs. Whitney would say if she caught me wandering around up here in the middle of the night. Thank you for a wonderful time."

Mark bent his head and his lips on hers were gentle and undemanding. She was enjoying the pleasing sensation when suddenly the room was bright with a blinding light and a voice filled with scorn rasped behind them.

"So you're finally back! I'd about decided you were spending the night in a motel somewhere!"

Karen and Mark sprang apart, shocked by the unexpected intrusion and the unjust accusation. Karen's voice squeaked as she gasped. "Mr. McKittrick!"

Shane glared at her. "Oh, so you do remember me! I'm the one who hired you to catalogue my library, not seduce a member of my legal staff!"

He moved toward her menacingly, and for the first time she noticed the open door and the lighted room behind it. She noticed a large desk, covered with papers, and realized that he must have been working in there when she and Mark came in. She moved back, frightened by the look of disgust on his face, but he stopped and snapped, "I'd advise you to go to your room before I say something we both may regret later! I'll deal with you tomorrow!"

She turned and ran from the room, but not before she heard his words to Mark. "As for you, I can say what I have to say to you right now!"

Karen tossed and turned in her bed as she alternately seethed with rage and burned with shame. What difference did it make to Shane if she and Mark stayed out late? He hadn't even been there when they left. Had he been waiting up for them? It seemed that he had. He was probably upset because she had come in the front door. She should have insisted Mark let her go in by the kitchen entrance, but even that didn't give Shane the right to make such insulting accusations. Her face burned at the remembered words. *I'd about decided you were spending the night in a motel!* How dare he! How could she ever face Mark again?

At dawn she got up, dressed in a pair of tan jeans and a brown pullover, and made herself some coffee in the empty kitchen. She dreaded the confrontation Shane had promised. She hadn't done anything wrong, so why did she feel guilty? Was it because she'd shared a kiss with Mark? But that didn't mean anything—it was just a way of saying thanks for a wonderful time. She bet Shane expected a good-night kiss when he took a girl out. She shivered as she thought of Shane holding a woman's body against his, his lips seeking and receiving. Oh, for heaven's sake, what was the matter with her? The man was obviously experienced and she was pretty sure he didn't stand around kissing pretty girls in hallways. He probably took them to bed!

Karen ate her breakfast and crept silently up the stairs, hoping she could spend a few hours working in the library before Shane wakened and sent for her. If he was going to fire her, she wanted to get some of the books sorted and in proper order first. It was an extensive library and would have been a delight to work with.

She sighed and had started down the hall when the front door opened and Shane came in, wearing a windbreaker over his denim slacks and shirt. He looked different somehow—younger—in such casual clothes and he started visibly when he saw her there. His drawl was without menace as he said, "Well, if it isn't our petite femme fatale. If you've gotten up so early to see Mark I'm afraid it was wasted effort; I just put him on a plane for San Francisco."

She gasped. "You didn't—you didn't fire him."

Shane removed his jacket and hung it in the closet. "Fire him? Because of you?" He laughed. "You have an inflated opinion of your value, little one. Mark is a brilliant young lawyer and I need his services. I'm afraid if one of you has to go it will be you."

She bit her lip and nodded. It was what she had expected, so why did it hurt so to know she would soon be leaving?

Shane slipped his hand under her elbow and turned her toward the dining room. "Come and have breakfast. We'll talk later."

She hung back. "I—I've had breakfast already."

He frowned. "Are you being truthful with me? You're not skipping meals, are you?"

"Oh, no!" Her voice conveyed her surprise. "I never miss a meal—just ask Henri."

"Henri!" he shouted. "My God, have you been charming Henri too?" Karen stood there dumbfounded by his outburst, but before she could say anything he pushed her away. "Run along. I'll track you down later."

Karen was sitting crosslegged on the library floor making notations of book titles when Shane found her an hour later. He sighed with exasperation and spoke as though to a wayward child. "Karen, I'm not a slavemaster and you are not expected to work on Sundays. I've been looking all over the house for you. What are you doing down there?"

She looked up, instantly contrite. "I'm sorry; I thought you knew I'd be here. I just wanted to finish my inventory before I leave."

"Leave?" He shoved his hands in his pockets, drawing the denim of his light blue trousers taut across his muscular thighs. "Just where are you going? I thought you might like to take a walk around the grounds."

Karen's eyes lighted. "Oh, I'd love that!" Then she remembered and slumped once more over her notebook. "But I'd better stay here and pack. Is there a bus that will take me home?"

"Home!" Shane's voice was rising. "What do you want to go home for? I thought you brought everything you'd need for a month or so!"

She looked up, startled, into his scowling face. "But you said—I thought you told me I had to leave."

With an oath, he sank down on the couch and ran his hand through his raven hair. "I swear, you not only look like a child, you act like one!" He straightened and looked at her. "Karen, come up here."

He patted the cushion next to him and she got up off the floor and sat down, not sure what to expect. He turned toward her and took both her hands in his as he said, "Now listen carefully and try to understand. I was upset last night when Mark left with you and kept you out so late. I like Mark and he's an excellent lawyer, but he's also one of the most sought-after young studs in San Francisco and he's a fool if he thinks I'm going to let him use his seductive charms on a youngster like you."

"I'm not!—He didn't!" She stammered with indignation but he put his finger to her lips, signaling silence, as he continued.

"Be quiet and let me talk. I saw Mark kissing you and I know what he was leading up to."

"No! Please, it wasn't like that—" She tried to pull her hands away but he wouldn't let her go.

"Sit still and listen to me!" He was getting angrier by the minute. "I'm thirty-two years old and I've been around. I know what a beautiful girl can do to a man when she's in his arms and I want you to leave Mark alone. I can't afford to lose him to any woman—but especially to you!"

"I understand." Her tone was as stiff and unyielding as his had been. "You needn't worry; I won't bother you or your guests again. Now, if you don't mind, I have work to do."

He swore as he slammed out of the room.

Karen worked until her empty stomach protested that it was lunch time. She'd breakfasted early and in spite of her churning emotions she was hungry. It took a lot, she acknowledged ruefully, to ruin her appetite. She began gathering up her things when the door opened and Shane entered, carrying a picnic hamper. He greeted her with a smile, as if the angry words between them had never been spoken, and said, "It's such a beautiful day I asked Henri to pack us a picnic lunch. There's a spot down the cliff overlooking the ocean that's private and very pretty. We'll eat there. After all, I did promise you a walk. Now run along and freshen up; I'll give you five minutes."

She did as she was told, relieved that the tension between them was gone.

Shane was right—the grassy ledge a few feet above the waves lapping on the rocks below was a natural haven, beautiful and peaceful. It was protected from the cool ocean breeze by rocks and from the sun by a twisted cypress and several large flowering bushes. It wasn't far from the house, but the descent was steep, along steps that had been hewn into the cliff. Shane kept her hand in his as he led her down the steep path and caught her around the waist when she stumbled on the slippery steps. The small arbor was only large enough for two and they sat on the ground as they ate the cold chicken, potato salad, rolls, and red juicy tomatoes that Henri had packed for them. It was a happy lunch. They laughed and teased and talked of things that mattered not at all. It was as though they had just met and were getting acquainted, and Karen dared to hope that they would be friends after all.

By the time they had packed away the remainder of their lunch, Karen was aware of the ache in her shoulder muscles from sitting slumped over the desk and bookcases all morning. She stretched lazily and lay back on the soft blanket of grass. Shane smiled and stretched out beside her as she yawned and said, "Mmmm, I'm tired. I didn't sleep much last night."

He rolled toward her and propped his head up with his arm. The laughter was gone from his deep brown eyes. "Didn't you? Neither did I."

Her green eyes widened. "Really?" It had never occurred to her that he would lose sleep over a little thing like an argument with her.

He ran a finger down her cheek. "Really."

She liked the feathery caress and lay quietly as she said, "I'm sorry I upset you. Mark and I really didn't do anything wrong; we—"

His finger touched her lips. "We aren't going to talk about that anymore. Why don't you sleep for a while?"

She nodded and her weighted eyelids closed.

When she woke it was to feel his strong masculine arms holding her against his broad chest. She opened her eyes and saw that her head was snuggled into the hollow of Shane's shoulder and that her cheek rested against the soft blue denim of his shirt, which was unbuttoned to the waist, exposing a mat of tangled dark hair. She felt a surge of embarrassment. How on earth had she wound up cuddled in his arms like a baby—or a wife? He seemed to be asleep and she knew she should roll away from him, but it was so comfortable cradled against his length. Maybe she could lie there awhile and still get up before he woke.

She'd never been this close to a man before. Oh, she'd had her share of hand-holding and good-night kisses, but by the time she got to the age where other girls were getting serious about their boyfriends her mother was sick and she had little time for dates.

She hadn't realized how hard and angular a man's body was. Not at all soft like her own. She moved her hand and ran her fingers through the short soft hair on Shane's chest. He stirred and her fingers stilled but lay quietly against his flat muscular stomach. She felt the muscles under her hand twitch and glanced up to see his dark eyes looking at her. There was a teasing twist to his mouth as he murmured gently, "You'd better be careful, little one. I may seem old to you but I assure you I have all the normal male urges."

She jerked to a sitting position, her whole body ablaze with humiliation as she stammered, "Oh, I-I'm sorry! I—"

She looked away as he got to his feet, buttoned his shirt, and reached for the picnic hamper. There was regret in his voice as he said, "I'm afraid we're going to have to go back to the house. I have to drive to San Francisco this afternoon in time for a dinner engagement."

She'd known he was leaving, but now that it was time she felt reluctant to let him go. A question formed in her mind and she looked up at him through thick dark lashes as she asked, "Shane, will you continue looking for someone to fill that job you advertised?"

His eyes narrowed as he reached down to help her stand. "Yes, the advertisement will appear in the San Francisco paper again tomorrow."

She knew she should leave it at that but she couldn't let it go without making one more effort. She swallowed and plunged ahead. "Why won't you give it to me? Mark said I was the only one who qualified—except for my age. Is it really so important that I be twenty-one?"

Shane frowned his impatience. "It's out of the question, Karen. It's true that on paper you were just what I was looking for but that was before I saw you, talked to you. You're totally wrong for what I had in mind. Even if you'd been older I wouldn't have considered you—you're much too immature."

Her eyes flashed with frustration. "If you'd only tell me what the job is, what you want of the person you hire! Maybe I have talents you don't know about."

He grinned and his dark eyes lingered on her soft, quivering mouth and the rise of her breasts under the clinging shirt. "Oh, you have the proper talent all right. I'm sure you would be very exciting—"

He broke off abruptly and snapped angrily at her, "Leave it, Karen! I said no and I meant it! Now come along. If I don't leave within the next half hour I'll be late for my date."

Chapter Three

The next four days were lonely ones for Karen. Her work was interesting, but in the evening she had only Taffy, Jolene, and Erma to talk to. Henri was a family man and lived in Carmel, and Mrs. Whitney's room was on the main floor and she never fraternized with the rest of the help. Karen liked the three girls with whom she shared the servants' quarters but she had little in common with them. Taffy was closest to her age and the most outgoing, but she had a steady boyfriend who took her out in the evenings, so Karen contented herself with exploring the grounds. She wished she had brought her car. Mrs. Whitney had the use of a small compact from the car pool but when Karen asked if she might drive it Mrs. Whitney snapped, "The help is not privileged to drive the cars."

So much for any inflated notions she might have had about her relationship with her employer!

It was Friday morning when the peaceful monotony was suddenly replaced with frenzied activity. Shane called Mrs. Whitney to say he was bringing several guests down that afternoon to spend the weekend. All six of the upstairs bedrooms had to be cleaned and aired, and

the four bathrooms were to be scrubbed. Even
Karen was not spared but was told to pick up her
mess in the library and clean the room.

When she finished she went upstairs and
volunteered to help the girls. By midafternoon
all the rooms had been cleaned except for the
second bedroom in Shane's suite, and it was
locked. Taffy explained as she turned the key,
"This suite used to be used by Mr. McKittrick's
father and mother."

She opened the door and Karen gasped at the
fragile, feminine beauty of the room. It was
furnished with the blond Danish modern furniture so popular a quarter of a century ago and
decorated in shades of lavender and mauve.
Taffy hurried on, not wanting to miss the oppor-
tunity for a little gossip.

"This was Mrs. McKittrick's room, she was a
lot younger than her husband, and beautiful. I
guess he wasn't able to satisfy her, if you know
what I mean"—she gave Karen a bawdy wink—
"because she ran off with an artist. My mom was
working here at the time and she said the poor
old guy nearly went out of his mind—shut
himself up in the house for months and wouldn't
go anywhere or see anyone but his son. Mr.
Shane was only a boy then, and Mom says he
adored his mother. It must have been rough on
him."

Karen felt a stab of pity for the young Shane.
How awful to lose his mother that way. It would
have caused a messy scandal, all the gossip and
speculation and dirty jokes. She shuddered. No
wonder Shane was so quick to think the worst of
her. He probably didn't trust any woman!

She hated prying into Shane's private torment

but she had to know. "What happened to Mrs. McKittrick after that?"

Taffy shrugged. "As far as I know she was never heard from again. Her husband finally pulled himself together and managed to work himself to death. He died of a stroke ten years ago. That's when Mr. Shane took over the business, and he seems bent on doing the same thing. I never saw a man so wrapped up in his work. Even the guests he brings here are business associates." She giggled. "I'll bet all his women are stockholders."

Karen winced. She didn't like to think of Shane's women, whoever they were. She'd wondered why he'd never married. Could his mother's abandonment have soured him on women and marriage for good?

They changed the linen on the bed and Taffy looked at her watch as she said, "Karen, would you be a love and clean Mr. McKittrick's bathroom while I vacuum in here? It's getting late and the Dragon will kill us if we aren't finished by the time Mr. McKittrick and his friends get here."

Karen picked up the caddy filled with cleaning equipment and went into the bathroom. The fixtures were already spotless but she sprinkled scouring powder in the bathtub and started scrubbing. She didn't want Mrs. Whitney to find anything to fault. It was a large tub and rather high, the type a big man needed, but she was so short that the only way she could reach the back was to drape herself over the side, balancing on her stomach as she scrubbed. She was so busy concentrating on not falling that she heard nothing until an amused voice from behind startled her so much that she nearly toppled into the tub.

"Would you mind telling me what you're doing in my bathtub?"

She didn't have to wonder who it was—she knew. Shane was leaning against the doorjamb watching her as she landed in a heap on the floor. He reached down and lifted her to her feet and his eyes twinkled although his face was serious. "Have you been bathing in my tub?"

She could feel the hot color rise to her cheeks. "No, of course not!" Her arms tingled where his hands held her.

"Then why are you scrubbing it?" he asked reasonably.

"I—we wanted it clean for you." She felt like a little girl caught smoking behind the barn.

He lifted one eyebrow. "Aren't you aware that I employ a housekeeping staff to take care of that sort of thing?"

She looked down at her hands, reddened from the abrasive powder. "Yes."

His voice was no longer amused. "Then who told you to clean bathrooms?"

Oh, no! Now he was mad at her again and small wonder. She shouldn't have been so slow! Mrs. Whitney would be furious. "I—I'm sorry," she stammered, "I'm afraid I'm not very good at this, but I learn fast."

He swore and picked up her cleaning caddy and began shoving bottles and cans back in it as he said, "Karen, I have guests coming and I'd like to take a shower now, and unless you'd like to join me, maybe you should just run along and we'll sort this out later."

Embarrassment flamed through her as she ran out the door, banging it behind her.

There were people coming and going in the hall and an infant's high, insistent wail could be heard coming from one of the bedrooms. Karen was sure that her cheeks were still red and now there was the added humiliation of being caught among Shane's guests in her rumpled jeans and shirt with a red bandana tied over her hair. Mrs. Whitney would be furious!

She raced down the staircase, so intent on getting out of sight that she failed to see the woman in the hall below and ran right into her, knocking them both off balance. Karen sat down with a thud on the bottom step and the other woman grabbed the rail to steady herself, her eyes brimming with indignation.

"Why don't you watch where you're going?" Her voice was sharp and commanding and her eyes widened as she studied Karen. "Who are you? And what are you doing running around like a little hellion? If you're one of Henri's kids, you've no business up here."

The woman was beautiful, there was no doubt about that. She was at least five foot ten and slender as a fashion model. She dressed like one, too, in a softly tailored pants suit the same turquoise color as her eyes. Her short cap of hair was a deep mahogany that blended with her honey-tinged complexion, and the indolent tone of her voice indicated a snobbish lack of interest in the servants and their children.

Karen scrambled up and kept a tight rein on her temper as she said, "I'm not a child, I'm an employee."

The older woman's eyes studied her briefly. "You're new in the last couple of weeks," an observation that didn't seem to please her as she snapped, "Well, don't just stand there, take my bags upstairs to the green room."

She indicated a cream leather weekender and matching makeup kit sitting on the floor. Karen opened her mouth to tell the woman she wasn't a maid, then thought better of it. She was in enough trouble already. If she antagonized a guest, Mrs. Whitney would probably have her fired. She picked up the cases and carried them up the stairs.

The baby was still crying as Karen struggled along the upstairs hall with the heavy luggage. It was a howl of rage and Karen could almost see the dimpled little body turning red with its exertions. Poor thing! She wondered if someone was trying to calm it or if it was left alone in a strange house and a strange bed to scream its protest unattended.

She was so intent on her concern for the child that she didn't see Shane come out of his room until she was almost in front of him. He didn't look any happier than he had a few minutes ago as he demanded, "What are you doing carrying those bags around?"

Before she could say anything the woman's voice behind her answered, "I told her to put them in the green room, darling. That's the room I always use."

Shane's mouth hardened into a thin line and his eyes narrowed to slits as he addressed the woman. "Audrey, I'd like you to meet Karen Muir, and she is not a maid! Hereafter, carry your own bags or wait until I can do it!"

The woman called Audrey looked startled. "But she said she was an employee—"

Shane glanced at Karen, still holding the suitcases, then back to Audrey. "Karen is here to catalogue the library. Karen, this is Audrey Templeton and you can put her cases down. She can carry them the rest of the way herself."

Audrey threw him a withering look and exclaimed, "Really, Shane, you needn't make such a production of it. She said she was an employee. I naturally assumed—"

Karen wished she could sink through the floor. She agreed with Audrey—why did Shane have to make such a fuss? Why couldn't he have just ignored it and explained her position in the household to Audrey later? The woman apparently had a close relationship with Shane—she called him "darling." Karen told herself it was only her friendly interest in him that made her hope he wasn't romantically involved with this turquoise-eyed iceberg.

She put the bags down and tried to slip out from between them, but Shane's hand fastened around her arm. "I want to talk to you," he muttered.

The crying infant was sobbing so pitifully that Karen was getting worried, but it was having the opposite effect on Audrey. She rolled her eyes heavenward and swore in a most unladylike manner.

"Really, Shane, can't you do something about that squalling? You'd better tell Carrie and Ben to keep that baby quiet or none of us is going to get any sleep tonight! I don't know why they didn't stay home when their nursemaid got sick instead of bringing the noisy brat with them."

Karen was so appalled by the woman's insensitivity that she spoke before she thought. "But that's not just a fretful cry—the baby may be sick, or hungry! Is someone with him?"

Shane looked at her and nodded. "His parents are with him." He reached down and picked up one of Audrey's suitcases while still holding Karen by the arm with his other hand. "Come on, Audrey, I'll help with your bags."

Before he could take a step toward the green room Audrey stopped him. "Shane, that screeching is apt to go on all night! I can't sleep with all that racket right next door to my room. Please, would you mind if I took the lavender room in your suite?"

Her voice had taken a seductive, pleading tone, and Karen's stomach turned over at the thought of Shane and Audrey sharing connected rooms. She told herself that it was none of her business if Shane wanted Audrey within easy reach, but she breathed a sigh of relief when Shane let go of her arm and picked up the other bag, then started toward the green room as he answered, "Sorry, you know that room is never used. If the child doesn't quiet down soon we'll call in a doctor."

Karen took advantage of her moment of freedom to rush through the hall and down the stairs until she reached her room. She showered and dressed in a brown and yellow print pinafore with sandals on her bare feet. She decided to spend the evening either reading or watching television in the small sitting room, since there was a party going on upstairs. Mrs. Whitney came looking for her a little while later.

"Karen, the Tylers need a baby-sitter to stay

upstairs with their baby while they join the rest of the guests this evening. The child is restless and can't be left alone and I need Taffy, Jolene, and Erma to help with serving and cleaning up. Since you're not expected to do kitchen work, I'll assign you to the second floor to be of service to the Tylers. Hurry, now—Taffy will bring your dinner up later."

Karen realized that she hadn't been given any choice in the matter but she really didn't mind. She'd been worrying about the baby. Infants didn't cry unless there was something upsetting them and this one had seemed to be in real distress.

The Tylers handed their three-month-old son, Danny, over to Karen with almost indecent haste and left to join the other guests at dinner. She got the impression that neither of the parents knew how to care for a child. Poor little Danny, she thought as she held the fussy baby over her shoulder and rubbed him gently on the back, he'll be raised by nursemaids and governesses until he's old enough to be sent off to boarding school and there will never be anyone who really cares for him. She wondered why people like the Tylers bothered to have children, but, of course, it was the expected thing to do. Didn't everyone need an heir to the family money?

She unwrapped the infant and frowned. He was soaked! Not only his diaper but his undershirt and kimono. His mother had wrapped him in a clean blanket but neglected to change his dripping clothes. Karen undressed the wiggling infant and ran water into the bathtub. A thick bath towel in the bottom of the tub kept the baby from slipping as she once more balanced herself across the side and held the boy with one arm as she washed him with the other hand.

A noise behind her made her turn her head and look over her shoulder. She gasped in surprise to see Shane lounging in the open doorway. He grinned and said, "Do you spend all your time standing on your head in the bathtub?"

She laughed. "No. Only when there's something to scrub." She lifted the baby from the water and ordered, "Hand me that towel. No, shake it out and hold it so I can put the baby in it."

She set the child in the soft towel across Shane's arms and brought the ends together, wrapping the infant warmly. A somewhat surprised Shane was left holding the baby and followed her into the bedroom with him. She bypassed the bed and sat down on the thickly carpeted floor, patting the space beside her.

"Put him here."

Shane stared. "On the floor?"

"It's the only place there is to dress him," she said as Shane knelt and placed the towel-wrapped bundle where she indicated. "You didn't think I'd take a chance of ruining that bedspread, did you?" She indicated the hand-quilted satin spread on the king-size bed.

"You didn't have to pay for it," Shane argued reasonably, "why should you care?"

She shrugged and took a diaper from the stack of clean clothes beside her and folded it before she unwrapped the naked baby and began pinning it on. Shane watched.

"You do that as if you'd had lots of practice."

She jabbed a pin expertly into the folds of

cloth. "I have. I've earned my spending money by baby-sitting since I was thirteen years old, and you didn't ask my opinion but I'm going to give it to you. Women who can't even diaper a child shouldn't have one."

Shane spoke quietly. "I assume you're speaking of Carrie Tyler?"

Karen nodded. "I am. This poor baby hadn't been changed for hours. No wonder he cried so. His little bottom was all red and they didn't even bring along any talcum powder or baby oil."

She slipped a tiny undershirt over Danny's head and gently worked his arms into the sleeves. "When I got here she practically threw him at me and disappeared. Nobody could have torn me away from my baby if he had been crying so hard all afternoon! People who don't want to care for their children have no business having them!"

Shane started visibly, then was silent while Karen snapped the infant into his nightgown and pulled the drawstring at the bottom. She lifted the gurgling child and held him above her head as she spoke to him.

"There, sweetheart, now you feel better, don't you?"

Danny screamed with laughter and grabbed her hair with both hands and pulled. Karen squealed and tried to pry him loose but not until Shane got up and forcibly opened the clenched little fists was she able to get away.

"You're a menace, you little fiend. Now stay with Uncle Shane while I clean up the mess in the bathroom." She handed the baby to a startled Shane and left the room.

When she finished straightening the bathroom

Shane was sitting in a chair rocking the baby, who hadn't uttered a sound. She walked over and stood beside them, looking down at the man and the tiny boy. Shane was relaxed and seemed to know just how to hold a baby, and Danny was looking intently at Shane's square masculine face through round blue eyes. She dropped her hand lightly on Shane's shoulder and murmured, "You'd make an excellent father, Shane."

He turned his head and rubbed his rough cheek against the smoothness of her arm. He seemed about to speak but then the peace of the moment was shattered by a banging on the door and Audrey's voice calling: "Shane, are you in there? Karen, unlock the door?"

Karen hadn't known that the door was locked and she moved quickly to open it. Audrey stood there looking lovely in rose chiffon but her turquoise eyes shot sparks as she snapped, "Have you seen Mr. McKittrick?" Her mouth dropped open as Shane came up behind Karen, still carrying the baby. She uttered a strangled sound and said, "Shane, Mrs. Whitney has had dinner ready to serve for the past half hour and nobody knew where you were. I certainly didn't expect to find you here. What's the matter? Isn't Karen capable of looking after the child by herself?"

Shane handed Karen the sleeping child and spoke to Audrey. "I'm sorry Mrs. Whitney has been inconvenienced. Tell her to go ahead and prepare to serve; I'll be down in a few minutes." He shut the door quietly but firmly in Audrey's face.

Karen turned to walk away, but his hands on

her shoulders stopped her. "Karen, it was never my intention for you to baby-sit. I didn't even know that's what you were doing until I asked Mrs. Whitney where you were and she told me. Who sent you up here?"

There was anger in his voice and Karen didn't want to cause trouble by admitting that Mrs. Whitney hadn't given her much choice in the matter so she said, "I volunteered to come. I was worried about the baby, afraid it might be sick from crying so hard. Besides, the other girls were needed to help with the dinner party. I didn't have anything else to do."

"Of course you had something else to do," he said irritably. "You were supposed to join the rest of us at dinner."

Karen turned to face him. "But I didn't know that, Shane."

His face twisted in disgust. "I swear, Karen, if I didn't know you better I'd think you were simpleminded! Where did you expect to eat?"

Karen knew she'd better get Shane downstairs or Audrey would be up again and Mrs. Whitney would be furious. She put her finger to her lips in a shushing motion.

"Please, you'll wake the baby. Go on down to your guests. I'll be fine. One of the girls will bring my dinner on a tray."

Shane swore and stalked out of the room.

Little Danny snuggled down and went right to sleep when Karen put him in the portable crib, the only piece of equipment his disinterested parents had thought to bring, and Taffy came almost immediately with Karen's supper tray. She knew that must have been Shane's doing, otherwise Mrs. Whitney would have waited until dinner was over before bothering to remember her. As the evening wore on she curled up in the chair with a book. She was tired after cleaning house most of the day and before long the words on the page began to blur and her head dropped against the soft upholstery.

It was much later when she heard voices speaking quietly in the room but she couldn't seem to wake up enough to open her eyes. She stirred and was aware of an arm around her shoulders and another under her knees, lifting her up. She knew it was Shane. She could tell by the spicy smell of him, and the feel of him, and the way she fitted against him as if she were meant to be there. She wound her arms around his neck and buried her face in his shoulder as he started across the room. She couldn't let him carry her down all those stairs but it wouldn't hurt to snuggle close against him until they got out in the hall. Shane said good night to the Tylers and walked through the door with her when a high-pitched shreak tore through the silence.

"Shane!" There was no mistaking Audrey's voice. "Where are you going with her?"

Karen jumped, then stiffened, and Shane put her down on her feet, then turned to Audrey. "For heaven's sake, Audrey, keep it down! Do you want to wake the baby?"

Audrey shot Karen a murderous glance but spoke sweetly to Shane. "Sorry, darling, but I can't get my window open. It's stuck and you know I can't sleep without fresh air."

Karen wondered how Shane would know that unless—Shut up, she told herself, it was none of her business *what* he did.

Shane still had his arm around Karen's waist as he answered, "I'll come look at it as soon as I see Karen to her room."

Karen pulled abruptly away from him. Who was she to keep him from the beautiful Audrey's side? She smiled thinly at him as she stepped away and said, "Thank you, but I'll be all right," then scurried off toward the stairway before he could stop her.

She was wakened from a deep sleep by a pounding on her door and an angry male voice calling. "Karen, wake up and open this door or I'll use my key!"

She opened her eyes and sprang to a sitting position. The faint light of dawn peeked through her drawn drapes as the pounding started again. She jumped out of bed and, forgetting the low-cut, revealing blue nightgown she wore, raced to open the door, switching on the light as she did so.

It was Shane, in a long wine velour robe, eyes blazing with rage as he swept past her into the room. She glimpsed Mrs. Whitney in a navy blue robe standing in the hall. Karen cowered back and Shane towered over her, his mouth twisted in uncontrolled fury. What had she done now? How could she have made him so angry when she'd been asleep?

His voice was low as he growled, "How long have you been sleeping down here?"

She was too surprised to answer with anything but the truth. "I've always slept down here—you know that."

"Know that!" he almost shouted. "I know no such thing! I thought you had the room across from mine. I wondered why I never heard or saw you upstairs—" He stopped as if something had just occurred to him. "Is that why you wouldn't take your meals with me? Did she"—he motioned to Mrs. Whitney, who was now hurrying down the hall—"tell you to eat down here?"

Karen nodded, unable or possibly unwilling to lie to protect the housekeeper. Shane groaned and took her small oval face in his hands, tilting it until she was looking straight into his dark brown eyes, eyes that were still clouded with anger.

"Karen, I can't tell you how upset I am to find that you have been treated so shamefully in my home. You were to be regarded as a guest, and Mrs. Whitney knew that. I'll deal with her later, but I'm telling you now, you are to have complete freedom of the house and grounds and the use of anything you need, including the cars. You are not an employee; you are a guest who is doing me a favor by putting my library in order. In appreciation I am paying you a reasonable stipend for your valuable service. Is that clear?"

She nodded, her eyes on his expressive face and the sensuous mouth that was saying such wonderful things. He bent his head and brushed her lips lightly with his then took them in a hungry kiss, sending shock waves of emotion through her. His hands left her face and drew her to him, burning through her silky gown wherever they touched. Her arms rose of their own accord and wound around his neck, her fingers caressing the back of his dark head. As his tongue found the sweetness of her parted mouth she shivered, and with a groan he pushed her away. His voice trembled as he said, "You'd better put some clothes on."

He turned away from her as she reached for her gingham robe and his voice was under control when he spoke again.

"I almost forgot the reason I was looking for you in the first place. The baby is crying again and Carrie doesn't seem to have the vaguest idea how to calm him. The whole household is probably awake by now. Would you mind—?"

"Of course not. The poor little guy's probably hungry. I'll warm his bottle and take it with me."

Mrs. Whitney was not in evidence but Karen wondered uneasily if she had lingered to watch the kiss. Shane had said she'd have no more trouble from the woman, but Karen wasn't so sure—something about Mrs. Whitney frightened her, made her feel like a backward child who wasn't performing up to expectations.

They climbed the stairs to the small kitchen next to the dining room, where Karen stopped to warm a bottle. Shane told her to take the baby to his room and feed it, then went in search of Mrs. Whitney.

Ben Tyler was pacing the floor of the room with the screaming child while Carrie huddled on the bed in tears. Karen took the unhappy baby from his relieved father, gathered up a pile of clean clothes, and walked across the hall and down a few doors to Shane's room. She changed the infant's wet clothes and settled down in the big armchair to feed him.

It was quiet and peaceful in this big, masculine room, and it was plainly evident that no woman shared it on a continuing basis. It was decorated in moss, ocher, and ecru—earth tones that complemented the dark, heavy furniture. Gleaming brass lamps added a lighter touch, and a large oil painting of a sailing ship, by an artist whose name was unfamiliar to Karen, provided the only bright color.

A glance at the bottle told her the baby had already taken two ounces of his formula and she pulled the nipple from his mouth and put him over her shoulder, gently rubbing her hand upward on his back to relieve the inevitable bubble of gas.

The door opened and Shane entered. His long wine robe parted at the bottom as he walked, revealing no trace of pajamas underneath. He smiled at Karen and sat down on the side of the bed as he said, "Your things are being moved to the room across the hall and I don't ever want to catch you in the servants' quarters again." She started to protest that it could have waited till later but he hurried on. "Mrs. Whitney insists she misunderstood my orders about how you were to be treated and I confess I'm at a loss to understand why she would do such a thing deliberately. She's been highly efficient in the past so I told her we'd let it go this time, but I want to know immediately if you have any more trouble with her."

Danny chose that moment to burp and Karen and Shane both laughed as the baby raised his small head and looked around, perplexed by the sudden attention. Karen cradled him again in the crook of her arm and offered him the rest of the bottle, which he grabbed with both waving hands and propelled expertly to his already open mouth. Karen giggled and said, "If he weren't so fat I'd swear they never feed him at home."

Shane lit a cigarette and watched her as she sat in the shadows of the dimly lit room. For a while he didn't speak and when he did his voice was husky.

"You're very good with babies, Karen. Do you plan to have a family of your own someday?"

Karen nodded. "Oh, yes, a whole houseful, and I'm going to stay home and take care of them. I don't want baby-sitters raising my children."

"And who's going to father those children?"

There was a tremor in his voice that struck an answering chord in her. It was a perfectly innocent question but the intimacy of the setting, the nightclothes they were both wearing and the memory of that kiss that had made her forget everything but his arms holding her, his lips melting her very bones, made her blush and stammer, "The—the man I love. I'd never give myself to a man I didn't love with all my heart."

"And have you met this man yet?"

For a long time she didn't answer, and when she did it was almost a whisper. "I don't know."

Over Shane's strenuous objections she had the portable crib moved into her room and took charge of the infant for the rest of the weekend. Shane introduced her to his other guests—all business acquaintances—and insisted she join them. When Danny was awake she kept him with her, depositing him on a blanket spread over the thick carpet, where he gurgled happily. His parents seemed content to let her do as she pleased as long as she didn't bother them about him. When he slept she made regular trips upstairs to check on him, and several times she caught both Shane and Mark watching her comings and goings.

Mark was paired off with the redheaded daughter of one of the older couples, who saw to it that he had no time alone with Karen. Shane and Audrey were a duo, and apparently one of long standing, and Karen'g dinner partner was an elderly man who seemed pleased that she was willing to listen to his memories of a long and happy marriage to a wife who had recently died.

On Sunday the party moved to Carmel with its artists' colony, galleries, and quaint little shops. Karen refused to go, explaining to Shane that she had to stay home and take care of Danny. Shane threatened to make the Tylers take care of their own baby but Karen was adamant and they finally left without her. The group was gone all day and returned only to pick up their luggage, and of course Danny, and head back to San Francisco. Mark had ridden down with Shane, and Audrey and they were the last to leave after seeing the others off. Mark and Audrey had gone to pack her luggage in the car and Shane was ushering Karen into the library for some last-minute instructions when the telephone on the desk rang. Shane answered it and handed it to her.

"It's for you."

Karen's eyebrows raised in surprise. Who would be calling her here? The voice was at first unfamiliar.

"Karen, this is Joe Voss with Valley Realty Company."

Recognition clicked. "Oh, yes, Mr. Voss—have you sold my house yet? I really do need the money as soon as possible."

Shane looked interestedly at her as the voice hesitated then answered. "No, I'm sorry. I'm afraid I have bad news. Karen, there's been a fire."

"A fire?" Karen felt the quickening of fear. "You mean at my house?"

Shane moved toward her as the voice continued, "It must have smoldered for hours before it broke out in full force. Honey, I'm sorry—the house, garage, and everything in them is a total loss. You have just enough insurance to cover the mortgages; there won't be a cent left over!"

Chapter Four

Karen stood rooted to the floor, her hand clutching the telephone like a lifeline holding her above the quicksand that threatened to pull her down and close over her. She swayed and Shane was beside her, his arm supporting her against him as he gently took the phone and spoke into it. She heard his voice but not the words. Images formed in her mind of the six-room ranch house that had been home to her all her life. The redwood and brick trimmed exterior, the neat modern kitchen, her room with Raggedy Ann and Andy print curtains and matching bedspread. And then her room with ballerinas on the curtains and spread, and, finally, the same room with imitation French Provincial white and gold furniture and curtains and a bedspread of yellow dotted swiss. Her whole life had revolved around that room. She'd studied everything from counting to calculus at the desk, had girl friends over to spend the night with her in the double bed, and curled up in the rocking chair to sob out her anguish when her mother died and again when she lost her father. The house was her only legacy, the bequest that would have kept her solvent until she could learn a skill and earn a living.

Now it was gone, destroyed! She was left with no past and no future—only a bleak and empty present.

But now there was Shane, his arms holding her, his fingers gently caressing her, and his voice murmuring words of comfort. His strength was a buffer against the shock and his warm, solid body shielded and protected her. It was then that the tears came. Not gentle and lady-like but great shuddering sobs that threatened to tear her apart. Shane picked her up and carried her to the big leather chair, where he sat down and cradled her on his lap, and she clung to him and cried into his shoulder. Someone came in once and Shane spoke to him, but she was too wrapped up in her own misery to notice.

Finally the storm subsided, the tears ran out, and she was too exhausted by her raging emotions to do anything but lie against Shane's comforting chest. His cheek rested against the top of her head and he carefully wiped the moisture from her face with his thumb. It was then that the door opened and Mark came in. He eyed Karen cuddled in Shane's lap but spoke to Shane.

"Is she all right?"

Shane's eyebrows raised. "I thought I told you to take one of the cars and drive Audrey back to San Francisco."

It must have been Mark who came in earlier when she was too devastated to pay attention. Mark slumped down on the red velour couch and said, "I put her in a car and told her to drive herself home. I think I know what you're planning and I want to be here to protect Karen's rights."

Shane stiffened. "You think she needs protection from me?"

Mark nodded grimly. "I do. I went along with this harebrained scheme of yours because I thought you'd pick a woman as hard and practical as you are. One who's selfish enough to put money and her own creature comforts above everything else, but Karen's a lamb being led to the slaughter and I'm not going to stand for it."

"What are you two talking about?" Karen asked.

Neither man paid the slightest attention to her question as Shane, his voice cold and haughty, said to Mark, "You know I don't have to stand for your insults."

"I know I could lose my job," Mark acknowledged. "I like working for you but there are some things I won't be a party to. Fire me if you must but I intend to represent Karen in this folly."

Now they definitely had Karen's attention and she sat up, puzzled. "Represent me in what, Mark? Why do I need a lawyer? You mean because my house burned down?"

Mark snorted. "No, I mean because of the proposition Shane's about to put to you. That so-called job he advertised in the paper."

Karen turned to look at Shane. "You mean you're going to give me the job after all?"

Oh, please say yes! she pleaded silently. If he would just let her work for him on a permanent basis her troubles would be over. Why was Mark so against it? He knew how badly she needed the job and still he fought against Shane giving it to her. If Shane thought she could fill it what business was it of Mark's?

Shane's arms tightened around her waist as if

he was afraid she'd slide off his lap, but there was a hard finality in his voice. "No, Karen, I am not going to give you the job and this blundering idiot had no right to assume I would! I've told you over and over again, that position is not for you. If I told you what it is you wouldn't even want it—now forget it!"

Forget it! How *could* she forget it, when it seemed to be her only option? What was it Shane wanted of the woman he advertised for? Why was Mark in favor of it for someone else but not for her? What was going on here anyway?

"But why, Shane?" she cried. "Why are you so sure I couldn't do it? Why do you think I *wouldn't* do it? Why won't you tell me what it is so I can make up my own mind? I'm not a child and I have to find some way to support myself. When I leave here I won't even have enough money to eat on."

"Oh, for heaven's sake, little one." Shane sighed with exasperation. "I'm not going to let you starve! I'll send you to school. Decide where you want to go and I'll pay for it as well as give you an allowance while you're there."

Karen was stunned. "But why should you do that? I'm nothing to you and I'm not a charity case. I won't take your money unless I work for it!"

Shane swore and set her on her feet as he got up from the chair and began pacing the room. "All right, damn it, I'll tell you what the job is, but this is highly confidential and you are never to breathe a word of it to anyone! Understand?"

She nodded, dumbfounded by his change of mind and his vehemence. He stopped his pacing and looked at her. "I need a woman, a stranger, who for a large sum of money will marry me and give me a child." Karen gasped but he continued. "Once the child is born she must agree to divorce me and give me sole custody of my son."

Karen stared, shock registered on her open mouth and in her round, unblinking eyes. The man was out of his mind! Stark raving mad! Why would a man like Shane, who could have any woman he wanted, advertise for a wife?

He was standing there watching her, waiting for her reaction, which wasn't long in coming. "You've got to be kidding!"

He shook his head. "I've never been more serious. I need an heir to carry on the family business."

"But there must be dozens of women who would jump at the chance to be your wife."

He uttered a short bitter laugh. "I don't want a wife—just a woman with good breeding and background who will give me a son."

"Then why marry her? Why don't you just pay her to have your baby?"

"My son must be legitimate." His tone was harsh.

"Your moral concern is touching." Her voice dripped sarcasm. "And how can you be so sure it will be a son?"

"Morals have nothing to do with it," he snapped. "I want no legal clouding of the issue once the child is old enough to take over the company. As to the sex of the baby, there hasn't been a girl child in my father's family in over one hundred years, and since I'm the one who 'decides' that issue . . ." He shrugged. "It's not foolproof, but it does make it more likely that any child of mine would be a son."

Karen could see that she was no match for his verbal sparring and turned to look at Mark, still seated on the sofa watching them. "Mark, he's teasing isn't he? I don't think it's a bit funny. I think it's beastly of both of you!"

Mark looked up and his eyes locked with hers. "No, Karen, he's not teasing. That's exactly what he's advertising for, a woman who can be bought and discarded."

Shane winced. "Oh, come off it, Mark! All she has to give me is one year—maybe less if she's quick about it—and then she's free and will be financially secure for the rest of her life. It's a hell of a lot better than getting starry-eyed over the local garage mechanic and wasting her youth having a baby every other year and trying to make the paycheck stretch from one month to the next."

Karen dropped back down in the leather chair, shattered by his callous contempt. She knew she shouldn't ask the question forming in her mind but she had to know. "Why do you hate women, Shane?"

He looked genuinely surprised. "Hate them? I don't hate them. I'm very fond of them—ask anybody. I use them and they use me and we get along just fine as long as I have the good sense not to marry one and expect the marriage to be happy and long lasting."

Karen shifted miserably in the chair. Shane was right, she wouldn't accept the position if it were offered.

Mark was the first to break the shocked si-

lence. He'd been watching Karen and his voice
was soft as he spoke. "You look as though you'd
lost your last friend, honey. You haven't, you
know. You still have me." He stood and walked
over to her. "You need to get away from here for
a while, try to forget the things that have
happened today. Come on. Go wash that pretty
little tear-ravaged face and I'll take you out to
dinner and a movie."

She looked up, puzzled. "But aren't you and
Shane going back to San Francisco?"

Shane answered. "No. Not tonight. Go with
Mark and enjoy yourself and tomorrow we'll
take you back to your hometown and make
whatever arrangements have to be made about
the fire."

Afterward Karen knew it would have taken
her days to handle all the business details that
Mark and Shane took care of in a few hours.
They insisted on seeing the burned-out ruin of
her house and talking to the police about it. They
were told that the police suspected vandals had
set the fire either accidentally or deliberately to
cover their mischief. Everything was gone—
even her car, which had been in the garage.
Shane and Mark were closeted with the realtor
for almost an hour and she was called in only
when there were papers to sign. She suspected
that there had been a few debts that Shane had
paid but he refused to discuss it and, anyway,
there was nothing she could do about it now. It
just put her further into his debt.

On Tuesday, Shane and Mark dropped Karen
at the house and went back to San Francisco,
and Karen had her first confrontation with Mrs.
Whitney since the unpleasantness over her

room. When Mrs. Whitney came to announce in stiff, formal tones that dinner was ready to be served Karen said, "Oh, Mrs. Whitney, it's not necessary to serve my meals in the dining room when I'm here alone. I'll eat in the kitchen with the rest of you."

Mrs. Whitney's lips pressed together and her voice was filled with disdain as she spoke. "I'm sorry, Miss, I couldn't possibly allow that. Mr. McKittrick left specific orders that you are a guest. It would never do for you to take your meals with the servants. If you would like to be seated I will serve the first course."

Her words were servile, exaggeratedly respectful, but she made no attempt to hide the hate that shone from her eyes. Karen knew she had made an enemy—a dangerous one!

On Friday, Shane and Mark came back. This time Karen was not scrubbing Shane's bathtub when he got there but pacing up and down the front porch, dodging hanging baskets of begonias and wishing she could calm down and be cool and collected. She'd spent her days working hard so she wouldn't have to think, but by evening her eyes burned too badly to continue her cataloguing and she had nothing to do but ponder over Shane and his preposterous proposal. He wasn't proposing to *her* so why should she lose sleep over it? But she did. Part of the time she was incensed at his callousness. At other times she was filled with compassion for the man who had been hurt so badly by his mother's desertion that it warped his whole attitude toward women. But worst of all were the times when her undisciplined mind dwelt on the woman he would choose for the mother of his child. She would be like Audrey, tall and curvacious, beautiful and well educated with a pedigree like a show dog. In her mind's eye she could see Shane holding this paragon of a woman in his arms as he slowly undressed her, all the while trailing kisses over the bare skin he was exposing.

She banged her head on the scarlet begonia for the fifth time and indulged in a few well-chosen swear words. It was then that Shane chose to swing his powerful car into the driveway. He ignored Mark sitting in the seat beside him and slammed the door behind him as Karen ran across the porch. He strode past her with only a brief greeting and went into the house.

After an uncomfortable dinner, they had coffee in the den, a smaller, more intimate room than the living room, and Karen could no longer hold back the question that had been tormenting her all evening. She was sitting at one end of the tan leather sofa and Mark sat at the other end. Thick fog, no stranger to the Monterey coast, had settled in with its inevitable chill and Shane had just finished lighting a fire in the stone fireplace that covered one wall and was sitting on the raised hearth with a margarita in one hand and a cigarette in the other. Karen drained her coffee cup and put it on the highly polished redwood coffee table as she said, "Shane, have you had any answers to your ad?"

He made no pretense of not knowing what she was talking about. "Yes. They've been coming in all week. Mark tells me there are more than a hundred."

Karen gasped. "So many! Have you—have you made a decision yet?"

She held her breath, hoping he'd say no, afraid he'd say yes. He didn't get a chance to say anything, Mark answered for him. "Fat chance!" he snorted. "I've narrowed the pile down to thirty who seem to be qualified but Shane won't even look at the applications."

"I've been busy," Shane snapped.

"Not so busy you couldn't have taken an hour or so to go through them and tell me which girls you want interviewed. I'd like to get the appointments set up as soon as possible." Mark took a long swig of his whiskey.

"Why do you insist on a stranger, Shane? You must know plenty of women with class and breeding who would qualify? Why advertise for a woman you don't know? Aren't you taking an awful chance?"

Shane ground out his cigarette and looked at her as if he wondered how she could ask such a stupid question. "None of the women I know would agree to my terms. They all have plenty of money and security and if one of them married me it would be because of the social and political advantages of being Mrs. Shane McKittrick. She might give me the baby I want, but she'd never give me the divorce."

He twirled the stem of his glass between his hands as he continued. "And don't lose any sleep worrying about my future wife's background. I had you thoroughly checked out before I ever came to see you and I'll do the same with anyone else I choose."

Karen couldn't believe what she was hearing. "But you can't get that kind of information without the person's permission!"

"Oh, come on, Karen, are you really that

naive?" His tone was bitter. "With enough
money and influence you can buy anything you
want. For instance, I know you had German
measles at the age of five, your mother's illness
was not hereditary, your father's heart attack
was a myocardial infarction and that you are
still, shall we say, 'innocent.'"

Karen gasped, struck speechless with shock.
It wasn't possible! Information like that just
wasn't given out without permission from the
patient! His last words echoed in her mind. She
dropped her flushed face in her hands and a
small shudder shook her. Mark reached over
and patted her knee; Shane reacted instantly.

"Leave her alone, damn it! She has to learn
the facts of life sometime. She can't live in a
dream world forever."

"You don't have to be so brutal!" Mark was
seething with anger. "There was no need to
embarrass her!"

Shane looked away and said almost to himself,
"There was a time when being a virgin was a
cause for pride, not shame."

Mark tensed, and Karen knew she'd better
change the subject or she'd have to deal with a
full-blown quarrel. Before Mark could retort,
she turned to Shane and asked, "If you insist on
a divorce and custody of the baby as soon as it's
born, who's going to raise it? A baby needs its
mother."

"Don't be ridiculous!" Shane exploded. "Look
at Carrie Tyler and little Danny. You told me
yourself that she was a rotten mother. The child
was much better off with you, the baby-sitter."

Karen cringed. He was using an extreme case
but she couldn't deny that some women simply

weren't cut out to be mothers. Shane was still watching her, waiting for an answer, and she said the first thing that came to her.

"That's true and Danny will suffer for it. I still say an infant needs someone to love it, and care for it, and teach it how to respond to that love and care."

Shane set down his glass so hard that it shattered on the stone hearth. He didn't seem to notice as he glared at her. "All right, I won't argue that point. But just because a woman has a baby doesn't mean she's qualified to care for it. I'll hire a warm, maternal woman to care for my child. In fact, that's a job I *will* hire you for. Would you like to raise my son, Karen?"

Mark sat forward and his voice rang through the room. "Shane!" There was a warning in his tone.

Karen knew Shane was being sarcastic, prodding her, hoping to find her weak points, but she wondered if he knew how badly that last thrust had hurt! She jumped up and faced him, unable to deal with the emotions that were building up in her as she said, "No! I'm going to have my own children. If you want me to raise your son, Shane, you'll have to marry me and make me his mother!"

She stopped, appalled by what she had just suggested. The tension mounted as both Shane and Mark stared at her, open mouthed with amazement. What was the matter with her? How could she even think about taking part in Shane's monsterous scheme, let alone talk about it? She would never marry knowing ahead of time that it would end in divorce. If she loved a man she would want to be married to him all the rest of her life, and if she didn't love him nothing could induce her to marry him. But what if she loved him and he didn't love her? Would she be willing to bargain for whatever amount of time he would give her? Was she in love with Shane? She shuddered inwardly as the truth finally occurred to her. How could she have been so blind? She must have been in love with Shane almost since she met him—at least, since their picnic. She was in love with a man who would never love anyone!

She tore her gaze away from his shocked face and turned so she couldn't see him. Her voice trembled as she said, "Shane, if I had your child would you let me keep him with me. Would you let me raise him?"

A strangled sound came from Mark, but it was Shane's hands she felt on her shoulders, his body she leaned back against. "I might," he said huskily, "if you would agree to turn him over to me when he's older."

She turned to look at him and then she was in his arms, his mouth on hers blotting out all doubts about her feelings for him. She clung to him, afraid he would push her away, but he molded her to him and she could feel the quickening of his desire for her. The knowledge enflamed her and her lips parted under his as her fingers twisted themselves in his dark hair.

Somewhere in the background a door slammed and she knew Mark had stormed out, upset and angry. She didn't care, but apparently the same sound brought Shane back to reality because he broke off the kiss and nuzzled the side of her neck, his voice hoarse with passion.

"Don't tempt me, Karen. I'm only human and especially vulnerable where you're concerned."

He picked her up and carried her to the couch, where he sat down with her across his lap. She caressed his cheek with her hand and he kissed her again, this time making a determined effort to keep his passion under control.

"You'd be a fool to get involved with me," he whispered against the corner of her mouth.

"I know." She moved her head slightly so his lips were on hers again.

"Then why?" It was almost a cry of pain.

Some instinct warned her against telling him the truth—that she was in love with him and hoped that eventually he would love her, too. She knew he would send her away immediately. He didn't want the ties of love. All he wanted was passion—and a son.

His hand cupped her breast and she kissed the pulse that was hammering at the base of his throat as she lied. "I'm not sure. Maybe I like the idea of lifelong financial security."

She felt him stiffen and his hand moved to tilt her face toward him. "So, my little child-woman is mercenary after all. I should have known." The bitterness in his voice whipped her as he pushed her off his lap. "Well, if you want to sell yourself to me I don't see why I shouldn't take advantage of it. We should have a very superior child together."

She knew she'd hurt him but couldn't understand how. She'd thought she was saying what he wanted to hear. With a weary sigh, he leaned back and closed his eyes. For the first time Karen saw the lines of exhaustion in his face. She'd often heard him talking business with Mark and knew of the killing schedule he kept during the week, and last weekend he had entertained a large number of guests here at his home. Now she'd managed to upset him again. Maybe he'd rest if he were more comfortable.

She reached over and started to unknot his tie as she spoke, hesitantly. "Shane, I'm sorry. I don't know what you want me to say." She pulled the tie carefully from around his neck and unbuttoned the first three buttons of his shirt. "You've made it clear that all you want is a baby."

He pulled her into his arms. She snuggled against him and laid her head in the hollow of his shoulder as she started to unbutton his vest.

He stroked his long fingers through her tumbled brown hair and kissed her forehead as he said in a tired voice, "It's all right; I'm only getting what I asked for, which is more than I deserve."

His fingers under her chin lifted her face to his once more. His dark eyes searched her green ones as he murmured, "And, Karen, if you want to remain a virgin until our wedding night, you'd better stop undressing me."

Chapter Five

The two weeks between Karen's decision to marry Shane and the wedding were the most bewildering and hectic fourteen days she'd ever spent. First there was the premarital contract to be drawn up. She'd never even heard of a premarital contract before, and when Shane mentioned it, Mark turned purple and sputtered, "Karen's not signing anything without my consent as her legal representative!"

Mark used every possible argument to talk Karen out of marrying Shane. "You're too young—you don't know what you're doing! Shane will use you and then send you away, ruthlessly, without shame or guilt. If you're that desperate for security, marry me!" He paused as though startled by what he had said, then grinned. "I'm a little in love with you already. With a small amount of encouragement I could start thinking in terms of wedding rings and wet diapers."

Karen's eyes were wide with surprise as she stammered, "Mark, please, I—"

Mark shrugged. "I know. You like me but Shane's the one you love."

Her whole body jerked. How could Mark know she was in love with Shane when she hadn't even know it herself until yesterday? She started to protest but he waved a hand to stop her.

"Don't worry, Karen, Shane's too wrapped up in his own problems to know what you're feeling unless you tell him, but I'm not that detached. I know you'd never marry a man unless you loved him, and you're headed for heartbreak. Karen, listen to me. It's easier to walk out on him now than it will be a year from now. Don't do this to yourself!"

She was strangely moved by the eloquence of his plea. Dear Mark, he really was concerned about her. If only she had fallen in love with him! She smiled and her green eyes were bright with unshed tears of gratitude as she said, "Thank you, Mark, for caring, but it's too late. I'm already committed and I don't want to back out. If you really want to protect me, see to it that I'm guaranteed custody of my baby after Shane and I are divorced."

So Mark fought with Shane and his lawyer. Shane's first offer was to let Karen keep the baby for a year. Mark didn't even bother to discuss it with Karen. With a lot of shouting and table pounding they worked their way up, year by year, until they reached eight. Then Shane dug in his heels and refused to negotiate further. In a dangerously calm voice he said, "That's as far as I'll go. It's eight years longer than I'd give any other woman, and if Karen won't agree to it we'll simply forget the whole thing and I'll interview some of the other applicants."

Reluctantly, Mark brought the final contract to Karen. The divorce and settlement had never been in dispute and now Karen was faced with the decision of whether or not to give up her child when he reached the age of eight. She read it over carefully with Mark, then took it to her room and spent hours pondering over it. Eight years seemed like a long time—it was almost half her lifetime. By the time her son—if it was a son—was eight he would have outgrown his dependence on her. From then on he would need his father to teach him to become a man. It wasn't as if she'd never see him again. She'd have liberal visiting rights and Shane had agreed to let her have him during the summer vacations. She knew Mark had pushed Shane as far as he would be pushed. Now it was up to her.

The following morning she signed the premarital agreement and Shane began making plans for the wedding.

Mark left for San Francisco the next day, but Shane stayed, and Karen dared to hope they could spend the days before the wedding getting to know each other better, developing that special closeness that engaged couples should have. She was doomed to disappointment. The next morning Shane met her at breakfast with a pad of paper and a clipboard. Without even a handshake, let alone a kiss, he began the interrogation.

"Do you want to be married in the church in your hometown?" he asked.

Karen thought for a minute, then shook her head. "No. It would be too painful without Mother and Dad and I haven't any other relatives." She looked around and a thought occurred to her. "Would you mind if we were married here?"

He looked startled. "Here? You mean at the house?"

She nodded. "It's such a beautiful place. We could set up an altar in front of the glass wall and have the Pacific ocean as a backdrop."

He shrugged and made a notation on the note pad. "All right, if that's what you want. Is there a special minister you'd like?"

She shook her head. "Would you mind if we were married in a civil ceremony?"

His eyes sought hers as he said, "Are you sure?"

"I don't know any ministers around here and, besides, a minister would want us to go for premarital counseling. I don't think either of us wants that."

He chuckled. "You're so right." He made another notation on his pad. "Now, the reception. Do you want that here at the house, too?"

"Oh, yes, if there's to be a reception it should be here." She frowned. "Shane, will it be a very big wedding?"

He glanced up from his notes. "That depends on the size of your list."

"My—my list?" she said uncertainly.

"Your guest list." He sounded impatient. "There are about two hundred people I'd like to invite. A few are close friends and the rest are business associates who would feel slighted if they weren't asked. We'll send telegrams since there isn't time to have invitations printed and mailed, so give me your list no later than this evening."

Karen was overwhelmed. Everything was happening so fast. She had assumed that the wedding would be small, but Shane was talking about inviting hundreds of people instead of dozens. She sipped her orange juice as she tried to think. Her friends were all so far away. It was such a long way to drive for just two or three hours and then there would be the long drive back. Most of her school friends would be leaving for college about that time and, besides, none of them would fit in with Shane's friends—they were all so much younger.

Shane's words broke into her thoughts. "I called my secretary yesterday and told her to find out who is the most popular wedding consultant in the Bay Area and send her down here. Her name is Julie Warner and she'll be here about eleven. She'll take charge of planning the wedding, so if there's anything special you want be sure to let her know."

Julie Warner was a study in contrasts. She looked like a sex kitten and thought like an army general. Shane was delighted with his secretary's choice and spent the rest of the day closeted with Julie drawing up and discarding plans for a wedding more suited to a princess than the young daughter of a college instructor. Karen was allowed to stay around but they seldom bothered to consult her, and when they did she was so confused that she couldn't be of any help anyway.

The next morning Shane returned to San Francisco and took Karen with him. She was wildly excited as she and Taffy packed enough clothes to last her for the rest of the week. She looked forward to the two-hour drive. Maybe in the close intimacy of the car they could talk, make plans, learn a little more about each other. If Shane would just give her time to think instead of demanding instant decisions, she could tell him what she wanted.

Again she was disappointed. Shane turned on the car's magnificent stereo system and the semiclassical music that surrounded them was soothing and peaceful but made conversation difficult. She finally gave up and slept.

She was aware of the change in traffic pattern as they entered the city but was too drowsy to sit up. When the car finally stopped she opened her eyes to find Shane bending over her, his face close to hers, smiling.

"Do you always go to sleep when you ride in a car?"

She knew he was remembering the first day they met when she'd slept in Mark's arms on the way to Shane's home on the Monterey Peninsula. She stretched and he took her in his arms and nuzzled the side of her neck, sending shivers through her. She snuggled against him and ran her fingers through his hair. It was clean and thick and cut so that it followed the shape of his head. She kissed his cheek and murmured, "The first time I slept in your car you got mad at me."

He raised his head and looked into her solemn green eyes. "Mark was right—I was jealous."

She brushed a lock of raven hair off his forehead. "But you didn't even know me then."

"I knew all I needed to know." He kissed the tip of her nose. "I knew you were going to be a real threat to my nervous system if I kept you with me for long."

He lowered his head and his mouth covered hers. It was the first time he'd kissed her in the four days since she'd agreed to marry him but his kiss hadn't lost any of its potency. With a little shiver her arms tightened, and he pulled her closer as his lips forced hers apart and his tongue plundered her sweetness. One hand settled on her hip and the other found its way under her pullover shirt, sending tongues of fire down her spine. His fingers caressed her unencumbered breasts and the kiss deepened just as a horn sounded several times beside them. They pulled apart and Karen saw that they were in an underground parking garage and a car had pulled into the space next to them. The driver grinned and waved and Shane swore under his breath but waved back.

Karen pulled down her shirt and her eyes questioned Shane. "Don Sanderson," he explained. "A dentist who has the condominium just below mine. Come on—we'd better get out so I can introduce you." He sounded angry again, and Karen was once more at a loss to know what she'd done.

The condominium was pure luxury but on a smaller scale than the house. Shane employed a middle-aged couple, Gus and Bertha Hess, who lived in and took care of it. The living room window overlooked the Golden Gate Bridge, that miracle of suspension, and from her bedroom next to Shane's she could see the city laid out before her. Shane set her suitcase on the stand and said, "Change into something pretty. We're meeting Julie Warner for lunch and afterward she's taking you shopping for a wedding gown and trousseau."

Lunch in San Francisco was not a meal but an experience. The small bar, in an alley off the mainstream of traffic, catered to the discriminating and the rich. The diners looked like business executives with their expensive clothes and sophisticated manners. Both Shane and Julie were known and catered to and Karen felt out of place once again. The meal was good but she lost her appetite when Shane and Julie got so wrapped up in their conversation that they ignored her.

Afterward Julie took Karen shopping. Karen expected to go to department stores and try on dresses. Not so. The salon had no racks of dresses—just couches and coffee tables and acres of soft beige carpet. They were served coffee and cake while tall, thin models paraded around the room in every possible design of wedding gown. All of them looked too overpowering for her tiny frame but the elegant lady in charge picked two that she assured Karen would be exactly right when made up in her size 3 petite. Karen was doubtful but she finally chose one that she hoped would not submerge her completely. As the seamstress took Karen's measurements, Julie explained that it would have to be a rush job as the wedding was less than two weeks away. The brittle, sophisticated lady in charge nodded her understanding.

"Of course. You understand we will have to charge extra—the overtime and all—but we're used to this." Her fingers spanned Karen's tiny waistline and she said, "It would be better to allow for a little expansion right here, although she shouldn't put on more than an inch in such a short time."

For a minute Karen was puzzled, then she felt the blood rush to her face as she understood. She pulled away from the woman's grasp and her voice shook as she said, "I'm not pregnant! Now please bring my clothes so we can leave!"

The woman's face registered surprise and

Julie intervened. "Don't be so naive, Karen! So many of the brides now are pregnant that they even have a line of maternity wedding dresses. It was a natural mistake. She wasn't making a moral judgment."

The woman apologized profusely, and Karen decided that it wasn't worth making an issue of.

When they finished taking her measurements she dressed, and once more the models paraded before them—this time in outfits for the trousseau. Karen kept her order simple, buying only those clothes she would really need for the next few months. The only reason she was getting married was to get pregnant and she assumed that this would happen without too much delay. Then she would need maternity clothes, and since Shane was determined to get rid of her once the baby was born she wanted nothing from him but what was necessary to raise his child—his *son*, she reminded herself.

It was that evening that Karen finally had a chance to talk to Shane alone. They were having coffee in the den and he asked about her shopping trip. She told him about the woman who thought she was pregnant and his eyes darkened with regret as he reached for her and drew her close beside him on the couch. His strong slender fingers smoothed her long golden brown hair back from her cheek as he said, "My poor baby, I should have thought of that. I forgot that most people have minds like cesspools. I should have set the wedding date a couple of months away instead of a couple of weeks." His arm tightened around her and he pressed her cheek against the silky smoothness of his shirt front as his voice grew husky and he murmured almost to himself, "I—I couldn't wait any longer."

No, she thought bitterly, he couldn't wait to get this show on the road—to have an heir and get rid of me.

She pulled away from him and sat up. Might as well get on with the plans so there wouldn't be any delays. She cleared her throat and said, "Shane, I've been thinking about attendants. Do I have to have more than one?"

He looked surprised. "Not if that's all you want. Who are you going to ask?"

"Could I—could I ask Taffy?"

"Taffy!" he almost shouted. "You mean *our* Taffy?"

"Yes."

"But she's the maid!" He stared at her as if she'd lost her mind. "Don't you have any close friends?"

She knew she'd botched it. "Yes, but they're scattered all over the country at colleges, or will be by then. Besides, this was never meant to be a real, lasting marriage and I don't want them to think I can't hold a man for more than a year."

He opened his mouth to say something then closed it and his eyes darkened as he looked at her for a long moment. She was the first to look away and his voice was surprisingly soft as he said, "Karen . . ."

She had to stop him before he said something about her being too immature and she squeaked a little as she spoke. "Besides, I'll probably want to marry again someday and it won't make it easy to get a husband if all the boys I know think I failed with one marriage in such a short time."

The tender look was gone and his mouth was a hard, thin line as he got up and stood with his back to her. "So, you're already making plans to marry some young punk who hasn't two dimes to rub together and let me support both of you!"

She knew what he was talking about. The financial settlement they had reached included a generous monthly allowance for the rest of her life. There was no clause cutting it off if she married again. Her statement had been a bluff; she knew she could never love another man after Shane but she couldn't back down now. She sounded more confident than she felt when she said, "What difference does it make to you what I do with my life once you've taken my child away? You'll have what you want!"

His shoulders slumped and he ran his hand over his hair as he answered. "You're right, it's none of my business what you do once you're no longer responsible for my son." He turned and started out of the room. "Do whatever you like about an attendant. I have to go out for a while; don't wait up for me."

The wedding was set for the first Saturday in September at two o'clock in the afternoon and the day dawned bright and clear. Karen awoke at five. Last night Shane had insisted she take a tranquilizer before going to bed and she'd dropped right off to sleep, but she knew there would be no more rest this day. She got out of bed, pulled on jeans, a heavy sweater, and her walking shoes, and slipped quietly down the stairs and out of the huge silent house. She shuddered as she thought of the more than two hundred guests who would be arriving, as well as the extra help, the florists, the caterers, the musicians—

At least she wouldn't have to endure Audrey Templeton. Audrey, one of the bored, restless jet set had left on a round-the-world tour before the wedding plans were announced, and no one knew how to get in touch with her. Karen could imagine Audrey's reaction when she came back to find Shane married to Karen!

She determinedly shut off her thoughts and jammed her hands in her pockets as she headed down the cliff toward the grassy arbor where she had slept in Shane's arms. She shivered at the memory and wondered why she felt depressed. Why wasn't she bubbling with happiness? In a few more hours she and Shane would be repeating their wedding vows; tonight she would again lie in his arms, this time in his big bed, where he would make love to her. Wasn't that what she'd been wanting all along? Wasn't that why she'd agreed to this madness?

The steep descent claimed her attention, but when she reached the arbor the grass was wet with early morning dew, so she climbed up on the rock above it and sat looking out across the calm, incredibly blue ocean. There was no fog this morning—maybe it was a good omen. A wedding day as beautiful as this one must surely mean happiness. Happiness?

She looked back toward the house sitting like a castle in all its splendor amid the profusely blooming flower gardens and the rolling green lawn. For the next year she would be Shane McKittrick's wife and mistress of all she surveyed. Surely she should feel at least a spark of joy. Little Karen Muir, who had lived all her life in a house that probably cost less than the furnishings in one room of this house, would have servants to command, a fleet of cars at her disposal, and the doors of all the beautiful people opened to her, and she didn't have the good sense to appreciate it.

She moved restlessly and drew her knees up under her chin and wrapped her arms around her legs. What was the matter with her anyway? She'd gone into this with her eyes wide open. She'd shamelessly thrown herself at Shane until he agreed to marry her. She'd argued with Mark when he told her she was a fool. She knew beyond doubt that she loved Shane, so what was her problem? Surely with at least a year as his wife she could make him fall in love with her, too. She didn't really believe he'd want a divorce after their baby was born. She knew she attracted him physically, that was one thing he couldn't hide. Weren't lust and love almost the same thing? He liked her, was protective of her—he'd even admitted he was jealous of Mark—so surely it was just a matter of time until he fell in love with her.

But was it? Did she really know Shane? She'd thought she did, but in the two weeks since she'd agreed to marry him he'd been so distant. She'd hardly seen him, and when she did he was busy conferring with Julie or a caterer or a photographer. He was sparing no expense for this wedding, but was he really planning a wedding or was it a deluxe business party with a marriage ceremony as part of the entertainment?

She heard a car door slam in the distance and

looked at her watch. Six o'clock. That would be Henri, hurrying to set his pastry dough to rise so the early arrivals could have crescent rolls, coffee cake, and doughnuts with their coffee. Her stomach turned over at the thought of food. She couldn't be sick! Not today!

She slid off the rock and dusted herself off with her hands. The household was stirring; she'd better get back.

Taffy came to Karen's room at eight with breakfast for two and they ate on the balcony that opened off her room and overlooked the cove between the two jutting cliffs at the side of the property. Karen hadn't asked Taffy to be her maid of honor, knowing it would embarrass Shane, but there was no one else she wanted so she asked Shane to make a selection. He chose the young daughter of the federal district court judge who was going to perform the ceremony. The girl's name was Janice and Karen had met her just once, when they discussed the gown she would wear.

Shane must have understood Karen's need for a friend, however, because he'd promoted Taffy to be Karen's personal maid and companion. But she couldn't confide her fears even to Taffy.

At nine the florists arrived, at ten the caterer started moving in, and at eleven the first out-of-town guests were at the door. Karen stayed in her room, since she wasn't needed for anything; Julie and Shane were directing this production. She was not expected to put in an appearance until the familiar strains of the wedding march from *Lohengrin* signaled the start of the ceremony. She felt like the star of the show. The production revolved around her but all she was expected to do was learn her lines and show up at the appointed time in the proper costume.

At twelve the hairdresser arrived and set her hair, after which Taffy drew her a warm, soothing bath, and she soaked in bubbles for half an hour. When she got out of the tub she wrapped herself in a terry robe and the hairdresser brushed out her hair, then pulled the top and sides high on her head in masses of curls, but let the back hang free to well below her shoulders. Karen approved. It made her look older and a little taller. Next the hairdresser applied her makeup, skillfully adding color to her unnaturally pale cheeks.

At one forty-five Taffy helped her into her wedding dress. She was pleased with the way the designer had modified the original. It was made of a lighter weight material and had been stripped of most of the nonessential decoration. She stood in front of the full-length mirror and watched as Taffy zipped the long back zipper. A layered organza collar trimmed the scoop neckline and supplied capelike short sleeves for her bare upper arms. The overskirt, in sheer dotted swiss trimmed at the bottom with a row of white daisies, provided an apron effect and stopped just above the deep flounce that became a short train at the back. Karen was reminded of a milkmaid.

Next came the veil, wispy material that was attached to a coronet for added height and fell to the waist in back.

Taffy was ecstatic. "Oh, Karen, it's beautiful! You're the loveliest bride I've ever seen. Hey, don't cry, you'll ruin your makeup!"

Karen wiped at the tears that threatened to

overflow. She knew she was being silly but she was so lonely. All her life she had dreamed of her wedding day, always with her mother hovering over her, helping her dress, combing her hair, and her father, looking young and handsome in a tuxedo, walking beside her down the aisle. Well, today was that day but there were no loving parents or lifelong friends to share it with her. She was a stranger at her own wedding!

There was a knock on the door and her maid of honor, Janice, entered, looking radiant in delicate blush pink. She handed Karen a cascade of white orchids and fern. Her own bouquet was identical but her orchids were sprayed a deep rose.

The organ, which had been playing steadily for the past half hour, was silent. Then the tenor voice of the soloist, a friend of Shane's from the chorus of the San Francisco Opera Company, filled the air, accompanied by the now subdued tones of the organ. This was the signal for Karen and Janice to appear at the top of the stairway. The girls quickly peeked in the mirror then hurried down the hall, Janice first, Karen behind.

As they stood there listening to the solo, Karen knew that Shane and Mark, the best man, were standing at the bottom of the stairs, but she couldn't see them, nor they her. She was several steps behind Janice, who would descend the stairs first. The florists had lined both sides of the stairway with greenery and there were baskets of orchids at the top and bottom. So much beauty and so much expense, and for what? she asked herself.

The soloist hit a clear, high note and the song

was finished. Karen held her breath as the organist struck the first strains of the wedding march and Janice started slowly down the stairs. Karen waited for Janice to reach the third step then started her descent.

Now she could see Shane standing at the foot of the stairs looking up at her. She caught her breath. He was so handsome! The gray formal attire set off his dark good looks and he could have been a prince in this fairy tale setting. Her knees shook as she took the stairs slowly, bringing him ever closer. His deep brown eyes never left her, and if she hadn't known better she would have been sure that they were the eyes of a man looking at the woman he loved.

Mark, also dressed in gray, stepped forward and offered his arm to Janice as she reached the floor. Karen's green eyes held Shane's, and even through her mistiness she could see the open admiration he made no attempt to conceal. When she reached the last step he stopped her for a moment, took her pale face in his hands, and his lips touched hers with a brief tenderness.

She wished she could cling to him, but the moment was gone almost before it began, and he offered her his arm as they followed Mark and Janice into the crowded, flower-banked living room, where the judge waited behind the improvised altar.

The ceremony was short and with surprising suddenness the vows were said, the rings exchanged, and she was in Shane's arms. This time the kiss was mainly for the audience, warm and gentle but with little depth.

She stood in the receiving line for what

seemed like hours. Shane introduced her to each of his two hundred guests and her hand hurt from being shaken, her body felt battered from being hugged, and her feet were aching in her new white satin shoes. The bar was doing a great business and the buffet tables were loaded with food. Tables and chairs had been set up all over the house, since the air coming off the ocean was a little nippy for outdoor eating, and the roar of conversation and merriment almost drowned out the orchestra.

At first Shane kept Karen with him as they roamed from table to table accepting toasts and being proper hosts. Except for Karen's wedding gown, they could have been hosting almost any type of party. As the afternoon lengthened into evening Shane got caught up in business discussions and let her wander off alone. She found a seat in the corner of the living room, half hidden by stands of flowers, and collapsed into it. All these people seemed to be having a marvelous time at her wedding—she wondered why she wasn't. She was exhausted, her head ached, and the only person she knew in this mob besides Shane and the servants was Mark, and Mark was avoiding her.

She wished now that she had agreed to the European honeymoon Shane had suggested. At least they would be alone by now even if only on a plane. She'd had the quaint idea that it would be more romantic to stay here in Shane's luxurious home, where they could have privacy and get to know each other. Ha! Shane was as elusive as the fog that so often shrouded the coastline in the evenings and early mornings.

Just when she thought she could reach out and grab hold of him he wasn't really there at all.

She'd married a man that she didn't even know—a rich, handsome, generous stranger. Now what was she going to do? In a few hours, when he remembered he'd married her, he would take her upstairs and do his best to get her pregnant. Is that all their wedding night would mean to him? The making of a baby? He knew she was a virgin, but would he remember and be gentle, considerate, or would he think of nothing but his own satisfaction? He'd seldom even kissed her in the past two weeks—maybe he would ignore her tonight, too. Was he having such a good time with his guests that he'd forget his duties as a husband?

Karen jumped to her feet and moved around, trying to outdistance her thoughts. What was the matter with her? She loved Shane, she wanted to go to bed with him, so why did the very thought of his lovemaking make her break out in a cold panic?

She stood in front of the glass wall looking out into the lighted gardens. There were people wandering around out there as well as in the house. Would they never give up and go away? She glanced at her watch. Ten o'clock. Eight hours since she and Shane had repeated their wedding vows. She hadn't seen Shane for several hours, but it did seem as if the crowd was thinning out a little. She'd caught snatches of conversation all evening and knew some of the guests were going on to nightclubs on the peninsula while others would return to the Bay Area.

She leaned wearily against the glass but

jumped to attention as a hand on her shoulder startled her. She turned and looked into Shane's smiling face. "I think you've had enough for one day, Mrs. McKittrick." he said. "Besides, I can't wait any longer to have you all to myself."

The look in his eyes told her that he had definitely not forgotten his duties as a husband. Suddenly she didn't want to be alone with him. She felt safe down here among all these people. When he got her upstairs there was no telling what he might demand of her. She looked around and cleared her throat as she said, "But our guests. We can't—"

Shane's hand on her arm was propelling her toward the stairway. "Mark and Janice are taking over as host and hostess. We'll slip quietly away and nobody will miss us."

She gripped the railing as his hand at her waist ushered her up the stairs. She wondered what he would do if she hung back, but she couldn't think of a good excuse and he was capable of picking her up and taking her to his bedroom by force even if she did.

She hadn't been in Shane's bedroom since that night with little Danny, but now she saw that all her things had been transferred from across the hall at some time during the afternoon and the new snowy white sheer nightie and peignoir that Julie had insisted she order as part of her trousseau were laid across the turned-back bed. The lights were low and the soft strains of the music filtered up from below.

Shane took her in his arms and kissed her. She was stiff in his embrace and she turned her head slightly. Shane drew back a little and said, "What's the matter?"

I—I'd like to take a shower if you don't mind," she stammered.

His fingers under her chin lifted her face and his lips clung to hers. "All right, but don't be long."

She gathered up her nightclothes and rushed into the bathroom, locking the door behind her.

The warm shower helped to relax her as the stinging needles of water brought life back to her tired body. She wished she could stand there forever and let the splashing liquid drive away all her tormenting thoughts, but she couldn't afford to anger Shane. She was completely at his mercy now and she shuddered at the thought of what he might do if she tried to deny him anything.

She dried herself quickly with the big soft bath towel and slipped into the nightie and peignoir. They billowed around her like a cloud, concealing everything from her neck to the soles of her feet as long as she didn't take off the peignoir. The nightie, however, was low-cut and sexy. She brushed out the complicated coiffure and let her hair swirl naturally around her shoulders.

Shane wasn't in the bedroom when she opened the door and relief swept through her. Then she noticed that the French door was partially open and knew he was on the balcony. She headed toward it and saw him in the moonlight, leaning against the wrought-iron railing smoking a cigarette. He must have heard her because he turned and said, "Don't come out here—it's chilly."

He snuffed out his cigarette and came back into the room, his eyes cloudy with desire as he looked at her. He reached out his hand and she involuntarily took a step backward. He quirked one eyebrow and grinned. "Now that you're all fresh and clean I can't very well climb into bed with you till I shower, too, can I?"

She gave him a weak smile and he headed toward the bathroom.

Karen looked at the king-size bed. She'd never seen one quite so big. The sheets and pillow cases were yellow and when she ran her hand across them she found they were satin. Imagine her, Karen Muir, sleeping between satin sheets with a stranger. But she was Karen McKittrick now and Shane was no stranger—he was her husband. Then why did she feel this urgent desire to run, hide, get as far away as possible? Had she made a monstrous mistake?

She crawled in on the far side of the bed without bothering to remove her peignoir. Maybe Shane wouldn't notice. She lay down and pulled the covers around her shoulders. The mattress was soft and shaped itself to her curves, but she couldn't relax.

The bathroom door opened and she stiffened. It was too late now—there would be no more stalling, no turning back. In a few minutes she would belong to Shane, permanently and irrevocably, whether he wanted her or not!

He was wearing only a towel draped around his hips and he removed it before he got into bed beside her. He turned toward her and took her in his arms. He ran his hand across her shoulder, down her arm, and cupped it around her breast. Her heart was pounding but not with passion— with fear! Did she really want to give herself to this man who could arouse her so easily but whose only purpose in doing so was to get her pregnant—and then to leave her?

He nuzzled her neck and murmured, "Do you always wear so many clothes to bed? Don't you think we could do without four or five layers?"

She swallowed. "I—I didn't want to get cold."

His long fingers were undoing the tiny buttons of the filmy peignoir. "I promise I won't let you be cold. Sit up a minute and slip your arms out of these sleeves."

She sat up and took off the peignoir and Shane pulled her back down and buried his face in the exposed valley between her small firm breasts. It took real effort not to pull away as his lips took liberties that had never been taken with her before. Her hands tightened into fists as he raised his head and smiled.

"Is that nightgown stapled to you or can it be removed?"

Her voice wavered as she replied with a question. "Aren't you going to turn off the light?"

"No, I want to look at you." He was slowly drawing the nightie up around her legs.

She pulled away and snapped. "Please, don't do that! I—I'd rather leave it on."

Shane propped himself up on his elbow and his brown eyes searched her face. "Karen, what's wrong? You're trembling. Are you afraid of me?"

Afraid! How could she tell him she was terrified! Maybe if she did he would leave her alone. The hope died immediately as his hand resumed its exploration. How could she be so stupid? Shane wasn't a boy who could be put off with a promise of "later." He was thirty-two years old and he'd married her for only one reason—to give him a child. He'd have no patience with her if she pleaded for mercy.

She unclenched her fist and put her hand on the mat of dark hair that covered his muscular chest. "No, Shane, I'm not afraid of you." She tried to keep her voice steady. "It's just—well, I've never done this before."

He kissed the pulse at the base of her throat and murmured, "I know, sweetheart. I won't hurt you. Try to relax and let me teach you what a marvelous experience it can be."

She tried. She really wanted to please Shane but the more aggressive he became the more tense she became until he could no longer be patient and her nerves snapped and she began to fight. She pounded him with her fists and cried, "No! No! Leave me alone! I hate you!" and burst into deep, wrenching sobs.

Shane hesitated, then swore viciously as he rolled off the bed, snatched up his robe, and slammed out of the room.

Chapter Six

Karen's pillow was wet with tears when she finally fell asleep from sheer exhaustion shortly before daybreak, but she was awake again at eight with burning eyes and the heavy sluggish feeling of despair. She dragged herself out of bed and into the bathroom, where she washed her face and brushed her teeth. It didn't help and the image that looked back at her from the mirror was drawn and haggard with white cheeks, pale lips, and red bloodshot eyes ringed with puffy deep blue shadows.

How could she ever face Shane? She'd driven him from her bed and now he'd send her away. He was her husband and she loved him, but he had been right—she was too immature to be his wife, the mother of his child. She'd taken everything and given nothing. She hadn't seen him since he stormed out of their room last night, his patience at an end, his disgust unmistakable.

Karen dressed in a skirt and blouse, one of the outfits she'd worn to school last year. It didn't matter anymore if she looked like a little girl— that's what she was—too much of a baby to grow up and act like a wife. She didn't bother to repair her tear-ravaged face; there was nothing she could do to it anyway.

The cleaning crew was busy removing all traces of the wedding and Karen finally found Shane in the den, which had already been cleaned. He looked up from the newspaper he was reading as she opened the door and there wasn't a bit of warmth in his face. His icy glance returned to the paper as she came in and shut the door. He wasn't going to make this easy for her, but she hadn't expected that he would.

She walked over and stood in front of the fire that had been set in the fireplace. She was cold. The damp fog, absent yesterday, was back, but it was a chill deep inside her that caused her to shiver. She hadn't been warm since Shane walked away from her.

Shane rustled his paper and she noticed the silver coffee service on the redwood burl table. She poured herself a cup of the strong black liquid, more to have something to do than because she wanted it. She noticed Shane's half-empty cup and asked, "Would you like me to warm your coffee?"

"No." His answer was curt.

She took her cup to the fireplace and sat down on the raised hearth where Shane had sat the night he agreed to make her his wife. What could she say to him? How could she possibly make him understand when she didn't understand herself? She closed her eyes and took a deep breath as she said, "Shane, I'm sorry."

He was hidden behind the paper and there was no response. Was he going to shut her out completely? Not even listen?

She drew her knees up under her chin and clasped her hands around her legs. There was still no sound from Shane and the silence was unbearable. If only he would yell at her, swear, hit her—anything but this cold, stony withdrawal.

Maybe if she told him the truth about her feelings for him it would help. There was no reason not to—she'd already lost him. She raised her head and saw that he had put down his paper and was looking at her. For just a second, before he could hide it, she saw the pain that looked out of his dark eyes.

She licked her dry lips and her voice was almost a whisper as she said, "I love you, Shane."

She wasn't prepared for the rage that replaced the indifference on his face. He crushed the newspaper and threw it across the room as he shouted, "You'll go to any lengths for a little financial security won't you? Last night you couldn't bear to have me touch you but now that you've had time to realize that you can easily be replaced you tell me you love me. Well, get your act together, little girl, because it's an amateur production that will never hit the boards, and, please, spare me your lies!"

Karen cringed and her arms tightened around her legs. He didn't believe her! But then why should he? Her actions were more convincing than her words. She'd never make him understand but she had to try. She couldn't bear to have him think she only wanted his money!

She shook her head and said, "It's not like that, Shane. I want to make love with you. I have from the beginning, although I didn't realize it until that afternoon we picnicked in the arbor and slept in each other's arms. If you'd made love to me then, or the night I agreed to marry you, I might have been shy and frightened but I would have come to you eagerly."

He looked at her in amazement as she continued. "It's just that you changed so after we decided to get married."

He was calmer now. "Changed? How did I change?"

"You got all involved in premarital agreements and wedding plans and none of it seemed to have anything to do with *me*, Karen Muir. I got the feeling that any girl would have done— and it's true, any girl would have. You didn't want *me*, you wanted a mother for your child!"

Shane opened his mouth to speak but she hurried on. "I know, you told me in the beginning that's all you wanted, but these last two weeks you've just ignored me. I've hardly seen you. You haven't kissed me, or held me. You've seldom even spoken to me except to ask questions concerning our wedding plans."

Once more he tried to speak and again she stopped him. "The wedding was beautiful but it was too big and impersonal. There were hundreds of people and I didn't know any of them. Then we got separated, and by the time you came for me it was like going to bed with a stranger. I—I didn't know you anymore."

With a little sob she put her face back down on her knees and sat there, curled tightly into a ball. For several minutes the silence in the room was total. Finally she raised her head slightly and saw Shane slumped back against the couch with his hands over his face. He looked almost as tired as she felt. Was there any way they could salvage this disaster?

He took his hands away from his face and

looked at her, his eyes filled with tenderness and remorse. His voice was gentle as he said, "Karen, come here."

She got up obediently and went to him and he pulled her down on the couch and cuddled her close against him. Her heart leaped at his nearness and she sighed with relief. At least he wasn't mad at her anymore! He tipped her white, pinched face up and studied it before he kissed her puffy eyelids and said, "You look awful."

Her finger traced the lines around his mouth and at the corner of his eyes as she answered. "You don't look so good either."

"Did you sleep at all?"

"A little, just before daylight. Did you?"

"No, nor did I deserve to." He brushed her hair back and pressed her head into the hollow of his shoulder. "I've treated you shamefully, little one, though it was never my intention. I wanted to take care of you but I should have adopted you instead of marrying you. You need a father not a husband."

"No, Shane!" She jerked her head up and looked at him. "I'm your wife and I want to stay your wife!"

He kissed her trembling lips lightly and murmured, "We'll see. Right now we're going to catch up on our sleep."

He stood and pulled her up with him. When they got to the door of his room, he turned to her and said, "Don't be afraid, I'm not going to make any demands. I just want you with me. Do you mind?"

She squeezed his hand. "I want to be with you."

They removed their shoes and lay down on the bed fully dressed. Karen turned toward Shane and he took her in his arms and held her, close and warm but without passion. She snuggled against him and he whispered, "Go to sleep, baby, and, please, try not to wiggle!"

Karen woke to the hum of an electric razor and the splashing of water in the wash basin. She rolled over and reached for Shane but she was alone in the big bed. She opened her eyes and realized that he was making the sounds she was hearing. Intimate sounds that made her smile.

A glance out the window told her that the fog had lifted and the day was sunny and clear. The hands on her wristwatch pointed to one o'clock. They'd slept for four hours and she felt marvelous. She sat up and stretched as the sounds from the bathroom ceased and Shane came into the room. He looked freshly scrubbed and much more rested. She held out her arms to him and he sat on the side of the bed and kissed her. He tasted of wintergreen toothpaste and shaving lotion and his hands pressed her to him.

"Do you feel better now?"

She nodded. "Yes, do you?"

"Much." He pulled away from her and stood up. "The bathroom's all yours, but don't be long—lunch is ready."

Mrs. Whitney greeted them, then stayed discreetly in the background as she served lunch, but Karen could feel the chill of her disapproval. Without even saying a word she had managed to let Karen know that she thought Shane had been out of his mind to marry her. Karen had observed Mrs. Whitney and Audrey deep in conversation at times and she wondered if Mrs.

Whitney was disappointed that Shane hadn't married Audrey.

The housekeeper was quickly forgotten, however, when Karen realized that she was starving and attacked the fresh garden vegetable soup that was placed before her. She hadn't eaten since breakfast the day before. She had been too nervous to do more than nibble at the wedding and too upset to eat breakfast this morning. There were breast-of-turkey sandwiches to go with the soup and snow pudding with a creamy lemon sauce for desert. Shane watched her devour everything with wry amusement, but she noticed that he wasn't turning anything down either.

Later they went for a leisurely ride along Seventeen Mile Drive. At the Spanish Bay picnic area he pulled off the road into a secluded spot where they could sit and watch the breakers form far out at sea, then come rolling inward, foamy whitecaps riding the crest to smash and break with a muted roar against the shore. Shane put his arm around Karen and they relaxed against the cushioned seat back as he said, "I want to talk to you, Karen."

A stab of fear splintered and raced through her. Was he going to tell her he didn't want her anymore? Would he offer her a bonus for trying and send her on her way? She raised her face to look at him and he must have seen her fear because his jaw hardened and he growled, "What is it about me that frightens you so? I've never laid a hand on you but you look at me like you expect a beating."

She shook her head. "I'm not afraid of *you*, I'm afraid of what you might do."

"What on earth do you think I'm going to do?"

She buried her face in his chest. "I'm afraid you'll send me away."

His arms around her drew her close and she could feel his heart pounding beneath her cheek. With a little groan he spoke into her hair. "Karen, I don't even pretend to understand you. I thought I was going to have to convince you to stay with me and you were afraid I'd send you away. What is it with you? Last night you fought me, screamed that you hated me, and this morning you curled up and slept with me with no fear at all."

"I told you—" she murmured.

"I know." He sighed. "You're so damn young! I feel like a heel taking advantage of you."

Her arms tightened around his waist. "No! You're not taking advantage of me!"

His fingers caressed the nape of her neck. "Yes I am. Don't you know that if I had the strength to send you away I'd have done so that afternoon on the bluff, when I woke and found you sleeping in my arms. I knew then that you were dynamite and I should get rid of you, but I couldn't. I know now that the only thing I can decently do is have this marriage annulled and send you away to school. But I can't. You're like a fever in me that can't be quenched."

He lifted her head and his lips teased hers, then clung. Her arms wound around his neck and he turned so he could press the full length of her body against his. The kiss deepened as their passion mounted until Shane forcibly pulled himself away from her. His voice quivered as he said, "Hey, none of that! My self-control is gone after what you did to me last night, and there's something very important that I have to discuss with you."

She felt the old fear again and kept her eyes down so Shane could not see as she said, "What is it?"

"Karen, are you sure you want to go through with this agreement of ours? It's true I can't send you away but if you want to change your mind I'll let you go. So far, it's not too late."

She looked at him with wide, pleading eyes. "I want to have your baby, Shane."

There was a fleeting look of relief on his face as he said, "All right, then, we'll forget about the wedding ceremony and start over."

She didn't understand. "What do you mean?"

"I mean, my wide-eyes little innocent, that I'll forego my husbandly rights and court you as I should have done earlier."

She blinked. "But—"

He grinned. "Don't argue. I could easily be dissuaded! I'll move you into the other bedroom of our suite and we'll pretend the wedding never happened. We'll get to know each other the way we should have done before."

She couldn't believe what she was hearing. The sooner they consummated their marriage, the sooner she would get pregnant and he would have his heir. There was only one explanation and she could hardly bear to ask. "Don't you want me, Shane?"

He took her in his arms again and his voice was husky. "Oh, I want you Karen—never doubt that—but I'm not quite the animal you seem to think I am. You have to want me, too." He let her go and started the engine. "Would you like to go to a movie?"

They found a theater in Monterey that was showing a spy thriller and afterward they had spaghetti in a tiny restaurant, where their casual dress was suited to the red-checked table cloths and dripping candles stuck in wine bottles. Their mood was gay and relaxed and when they got home Shane helped Karen move some of her things into the lavender room that had been his mother's. He kissed her good night and left and she felt curiously bereft.

The next morning she made her bed carefully so the maids wouldn't know how badly she had failed Shane.

Shane greeted Karen at breakfast with a lingering kiss and the suggestion that they spend the day exploring the charming community of Carmel-by-the-Sea, a few miles southeast of them. Karen was delighted. She'd been to Carmel before with her parents, but Shane was a resident and knew the 'in' places where tourists were discouraged.

During the morning they toured the small but elegant art galleries along Ocean Avenue and had lunch in Carmel Plaza, with it's flowering garden and parklike beauty. Shane chose a French country café specializing in delicious Brittany crepes and omelettes served in true European fashion. They ordered a sumptuous concoction called a Niçoise Omelette, which consisted of fresh zucchini, tomatoes, green pepper and onion—all prepared in their natural juices then delicately combined with cheese. Shane drank wine but Karen couldn't resist the Café Viennois: espresso, chocolate, steamed milk and vanilla ice cream topped with whipped cream.

The breeze died down in the afternoon and the sun felt warm as they walked to the white sandy beach bordered by rare Monterey cypress trees. Swimming was prohibited because of the undercurrents, but they took of their shoes and walked along the icy cold ocean that occasionally lapped up around their ankles, then pulled back again, leaving their feet wet and caked with white sand.

They moved away from the ocean and found a secluded spot behind a boulder that sheltered them from curious eyes. Karen sank down wearily and Shane dropped down beside her. He took her in his arms and lowered her to the sand. It was soft, almost like a firm mattress, and his face was only inches above hers. He brushed the chestnut hair from her face and murmured, "Are you tired?"

Her hand caressed his cheek as she answered, "A little. I'm not used to so much walking."

He kissed her eyelids and the tip of her nose, then teased her lips until, with a little moan of frustration, she took his dark head in her hands and guided his mouth to hers, then held it there as their lips clung. His arms tightened and he rolled over, pulling her on top of him and letting her take the initiative. His cheeks and chin were rough under her lips but his eyelids were smooth to the flick of her tongue. His breath came in little gasps as she sought and found the pleasure points at the side and base of his throat. With a groan he rolled her off him and sat up, his knees drawn up under his chin and his arms clasped around his legs.

For a minute Karen lay there stunned, unable

to adjust to the sudden change. She watched Shane sitting there looking out over the beach, his face an unreadable mask. She sat up and cleared her throat before she asked, "Shane, what's the matter? Did I do something wrong?"

His look softened and he took her hand and kissed the palm, then held it against his cheek. "You were doing everything right, but my self-control is limited, Karen. Another few minutes of that and we'd have been arrested for outraging public decency!"

She chuckled and leaned over to kiss him lightly. "We could go home," she breathed.

The light in his eyes told her that he knew what she was really offering but he made no move to hold her again. Instead he said, "I'd like that more than you can possibly know, but we'd better not rush it. I can take cold showers for a few more days. I want you to be sure."

Karen wanted to tell him that she was sure, that she'd never been more sure of anything in her life, but she was too shy with him to put her feelings into words. He had every reason to distrust her impulsive offer after what she had done to him on their wedding night. No man would deliberately put himself through that twice!

The next day they went back to Karen's hometown to clear up some minor business details and give Karen a chance to say goodbye to some of her family friends. It was there that she found out for the first time what Shane's business was.

Ted Webster, their next-door neighbor whom she'd known all her life asked the question, and Shane answered. "We design and build boats. We have several medium-priced lines but most of our sales are in modification and custom-built models. We will either modify one of our standard models or design to the customer's specifications."

Ted, a boat owner himself, prodded further and Shane continued. "The business was started by my great-grandfather, who built a boat for himself. Some of his friends liked it and asked him to build boats for them and pretty soon he was in business. It remained strictly family for two generations, but by the time my father took over we had gotten too big and had to sell some stock to the public. However, the McKittrick family retains the controlling interest and it will be handed down to my son."

His son, Karen thought to herself with a pang. His son, not hers.

The next morning they slept late and then drove north on highway 1 to Santa Cruz, where they spent the afternoon on the boardwalk at the beach. It was a gaudy, noisy, raucous place with swarms of people, young and old, in shorts and faded jeans and damp bathing suits, milling around taking advantage of the last week before school started again.

Karen fully enjoyed herself. She had hot dogs and soda and rode the ferris wheel, ate hamburgers and rode the merry-go-round, and ate cotton candy and rode the roller coaster. They shared a seat on the sky tram and rode high above the boardwalk from one end to the other, then walked back by way of the games booths, where they threw balls at bottles, darts at balloons, and shot guns at moving targets, collecting numerous garishly colored stuffed animals as they went. When they'd ridden all the rides and played all the games, they put on their swimsuits and went swimming in the ocean. The water was cold and they stayed in only long enough to get wet, then stretched out on the warm sand and let the sun dry them.

When Karen's light skin began to turn pink Shane announced that it was time to go. Shane was silent during the drive home and retreated to his den as soon as he had changed. After dinner, he had more work to catch up on and some phone calls to make in his office, so Karen went into the library and started to work on her cataloguing. She'd left it only partially finished when she got caught up in wedding plans, and she was anxious to complete it. She loved the library and the floor-to-ceiling bookshelves filled with books.

The hours flew by and it was ten o'clock when Shane came looking for her. She got up from her desk and went to him and he folded her in his arms and nuzzled her neck as he said, "I'm sorry, I didn't mean to neglect you. There was more work there than I realized and time got away from me." He kissed her lightly and continued. "Would you like to go in the den and watch television? You mentioned wanting to see the movie—"

Karen hugged him and replied, "I'd rather talk. Can we sit down on the couch?"

They cuddled up together at one end of the red velour couch and Shane rubbed his face in Karen's thick brown hair as he said, "Was there something special you wanted to talk about?"

She nodded. "I—I want to talk about us. Shane, I—" She could feel the heat from the flush of embarrassment that was covering her whole body. She started over again. "I don't like the way we're living. I want to get on with our marriage. I—I want to sleep with you." The last sentence sounded breathless and run together.

Shane's arms tightened around her but he was holding back, seeming oddly reluctant. "Karen, I—"

She knew he was going to refuse her again and she couldn't bear it. She cut in quickly before he could go on. "I don't want to wait."

"Neither do I." His voice was husky. "But, believe me, it's best if we do. Now please, for my sake, go away. I promise you that we'll straighten everything out tomorrow."

Karen told herself she should be happy. Shane had said everything would be all right tomorrow, so why did she have this heavy feeling of foreboding? Why couldn't she hold back the sobs that shook her until she finally cried herself to sleep?

She slept late the next morning, after tossing and turning most of the night, and woke with a dull pain in back of her eyes. A glance in the mirror showed them to be red and swollen and her face marked with dry tears. She showered quickly. Afterward she did what she could to repair the damage to her face with makeup.

She poured herself a cup of coffee in the small kitchen on the main floor and Mrs. Whitney told her that Shane had gone, but said he would be back for lunch. She went outside and paced restlessly around the grounds, wondering where Shane had gone and why he hadn't wakened her and taken her with him. Why was she so uneasy? Shane had promised they'd stop this silly pretense of not being married, but he wasn't here. She wished she had someone to talk to. Taffy had been given a couple of weeks vacation after the wedding, but she couldn't have talked to Taffy anyway. She couldn't bear to have anyone know her marriage wasn't a real one, was never intended to be.

Shane returned at twelve-thirty and Karen ran to greet him. He scooped her up in his arms and kissed her with a hunger that put all her fears to rest—until she got a look at him. His face was pale and drawn, and there were dark circles under his eyes; his shoulders drooped and he looked exhausted. She gasped and brushed a lock of dark hair off his forehead as she asked, "Shane, didn't you go to bed last night?"

He shook his head and, with an arm around her waist, led her into the house. "No, but let's talk about it later. I'm hungry."

They made small talk while Mrs. Whitney served lunch, and Karen noticed that despite Shane's insistence that he was hungry he ate very little. When they'd finished dessert Shane suggested they go into the den, where they could talk. He settled himself in the big leather chair and looked at Karen, her feet tucked under her on the couch.

"Karen, I understand that before your father died you were accepted as a student at Vassar College in New York."

She was puzzled. This wasn't at all what she had expected, but she replied, "Yes. Dad was making the arrangements when his heart— when he had his heart attack."

"You must be very bright. It's quite an honor to be accepted at Vassar."

Karen nodded. "I suppose I am, but I studied hard for my A's."

"Were you excited about going so far away to school?"

She frowned. "Yes, of course. Shane, why are we talking about Vassar?"

He gripped the arms of his chair, but his voice was calm as he said, "Because I've decided to send you there. I'm going to have our marriage annulled and send you to school."

Karen stiffened. She couldn't possibly have heard what she thought she did. Shane wouldn't send her away—he'd promised! She stared at him with horror as she said, "No! You can't! I won't go! I'm your wife—at least until after we have a baby!"

He leaned forward, still gripping the arms of the chair. "No, Karen. The marriage has never been consummated; there will be no problem about an annulment. It's the only sensible thing to do! I had no business getting you into this in the first place. If you only knew how I loathe myself!"

He put his head in his hands and Karen went to him and put her arms around him. "Shane, don't do this to me; I know what I'm doing. I want to be the mother of your son. Please, Shane, don't send me away!"

He pushed her aside and stood. She watched him, too upset to speak, as he walked to the window and stood with his back to her. "It's all settled, Karen; I spoke to the dean. She says they will still accept you if you get there right away. I've made arrangements for you to fly out of San Francisco the day after tomorrow."

"Shane!" It was a cry of anguish but he went on as though he hadn't heard.

"I'll pay all your expenses and give you a monthly allowance for the next four years or until you graduate."

"But why? Why are you doing this? Just last night you said you wanted me!" She was fighting back tears.

A muffled groan escaped from Shane as he turned to face her. "Of course I want you, Karen! For heaven's sake, I'm a normal healthy male and you're sexy, innocent, and available! That's a combination that would drive any man up the wall, but, damn it, if I take you to bed I'll never get rid of you!"

"Get rid of me!" The knifelike thrust caused her to yelp with pain.

His face was a mask, devoid of emotion, and there was a certain cruelty in his tone as he said, "Yes, get rid of you. I don't want a wife, Karen. I told you that. All I want is a woman who will live with me for a short time and give me a son. And you're not a woman—you're a child playing at being grown up. You're too young for adult games and I should have my head examined for letting my needs warp my judgment."

His words were like a spray of cold water that dried up her tears and left her gasping with shock. What an idiot she'd been, throwing herself at him the way she had! She should have known he didn't want her after the way she'd behaved on their wedding night. His refusal to sleep with her after that was just his way of easing her out of a marriage that he realized was a big mistake. It was all her fault. If she hadn't behaved like such a child when he tried to make love to her everything would have gone smoothly; she would at least have been his wife for a year or so. But now she'd spoiled it.

She took a deep breath, trying to still the anguish that threatened to overpower her. At least she could try to save a little of her dignity. She wanted to stand up, but she was trembling so much that she was afraid her legs would never hold her. Shane had turned his back to her again and was looking out the window. She choked back a sob and said, "All right, Shane, if that's what you want—I'll go away to school. It's probably better this way. I'll have the security I wanted and I won't have to go to the bother of having a baby to get it. When will we be leaving for San Francisco?"

He still didn't turn around and look at her and when he finally answered there was a catch in his voice. "I'm glad you see it my way. I'm leaving now, but you stay here and pack. I'll send Mark down for you tomorrow. You can spend tomorrow night at the condominium—I won't be there—and Mark will pick you up the following morning and take you to the airport."

So he wasn't even going to see her off, tell her, "Goodbye; thanks a lot; it's been good to know you." She wished he'd hurry up and leave. She wasn't going to be able to hang on to her self-control much longer.

"As you wish. I'll be ready when Mark gets here. Goodbye, Shane—and thank you."

She hid her face in her knees but heard him turn and walk a few steps toward her. She looked up and their eyes met. He looked ghastly and she remembered that he'd said he hadn't been to bed last night. At least this was a decision he'd wrestled with.

He reached his hand toward her as if he might touch her but then drew it back and said, "Goodbye, Karen," and strode quickly from the room.

She was still sitting there, too stunned to function, two hours later, when Mrs. Whitney called her to the phone. The woman's voice on the other end was crisp.

"Mrs. McKittrick, this is Memorial Hospital in Santa Cruz. Your husband has been involved in an automobile accident and was brought here. The doctor has asked that I contact you, and he suggests that you come as soon as possible!"

Chapter Seven

The yellow Corvette tore down the highway at a speed far exceeding the limit as Karen fought to control it. She'd never driven a car with so much power before and, as usual, it was too big for her. She had to sit on the front of the seat in order to reach the pedals comfortably and in her haste she'd forgotten to bring a cushion for her back.

The nurse had refused to tell Karen anything other than that Shane had been in an auto accident and was being treated there. Treated for what? How badly was he injured? Terrible things sometimes happened to people in automobile accidents. They were torn, and broken, and crushed!

The car swerved sharply and it took all of Karen's strength to bring it under control. She'd have to stop thinking and concentrate on getting there without wrecking this car, too. The midafternoon traffic was heavy and she had to dart in and out of lanes to keep ahead of it. It seemed like forever before she finally saw signs indicating turnoffs for Capitola and then for Santa Cruz. Finally she spotted a sign that said HOSPITAL and she prayed that it was the right one. The signs led her through a maze of streets until at last a large building loomed up in front of her with a bronze plaque on the front saying, SANTA CRUZ MEMORIAL HOSPITAL .

Karen abandoned the car in a no parking zone near the large front doors and ran inside. The woman at the admission desk told her that Shane was in Room 316 and she ran up all three flights of stairs rather than wait for the elevator. Her heart was pounding and she was out of breath as she walked down the hall looking for the right room. She knew she should stop at the nursing station and ask if it was all right to go in, but she had come too far too fast to waste time now. Room 316 was at the end of the hall away from the nursing station and she hesitated outside. What would she find in there? How badly was Shane hurt? Was he conscious? She took a deep breath and pushed open the door.

The drapes had been pulled over the wide window and the room was dim. Shane was lying on the bed, which had been raised so that he leaned back at a comfortable angle. His eyes were closed and there was a bandage across his forehead but his arms and legs were unencumbered by casts so he must not have broken any bones.

She walked quietly across the room and stood by the bed. A lock of his hair had fallen over the bandage and she reached out and gently brushed it back. As she touched him, his eyes opened and he seemed to have trouble focusing on her, then he started visibly and exclaimed, "Karen! What are you doing here?"

Her eyes widened and a sick feeling engulfed her. He didn't want her, hadn't asked for her, didn't even know she'd been notified. She sank

down on the side of the bed and took his hand
and held it to her cheek.

"The hospital called me, Shane. I came as
quickly as I could."

"Damn." He jerked his hand away. "They
must have found your name on my identfication.
I'd intended to have Mark notified; there was no
reason for you to know about the accident."

All during the interminable drive from Carmel Karen had comforted herself with the
thought that he had sent for her, had needed
her, but now that she was finally here he was
angry because the hospital had called her. She
looked down at her empty hands.

"I'm your wife, Shane. I have a right to know
when you've been hurt."

He turned away from her, wincing with pain
at the movement. "Karen, this whole thing is
painful enough as it is. Let's not prolong it. I
explained it all to you before I left Carmel; now,
damn it, go back home and stay there until Mark
comes for you."

Karen stood up. She wasn't going to let him get
away with it this time. She wasn't going to be
ordered around like a child. She took a deep
breath.

"No, Shane. I'm not going anywhere. I'm
going to stay here as long as you're here. If you
don't want me in your room then I'll wait in the
lounge, but I'm your wife and I'm going to stay
with you."

He groaned as he turned his head again and
looked at her. His face was ashen and there was
a shattered look in his eyes as he said, "Do you
enjoy tormenting me? Now will you stop behav-

ing like a spoiled child and get the hell out of here! Go home and start packing, because I intend to see to it that you are on that plane the day after tomorrow."

She sank back down on the side of the bed and shook her head. "I'm not behaving like a child, I'm behaving like a woman—a wife. You're not my father, Shane, and I'm through jumping to obey your commands. Are you going to punish me all the rest of my life for what happened on our wedding night?"

Shane lifted his arm and laid it across his eyes with a weariness that tore at Karen's heart. If he didn't give in she'd have to. He was too sick to argue like this. His voice shook as he said, "I'm not punishing you, little one; I'm trying to protect you. You don't want to give your innocence to me. Save it for the handsome young knight all maidens dream about. Get out of my life, Karen, before I ruin yours."

He looked so miserable lying there, so white, his strength so utterly spent. She couldn't put him through any more of this. Suddenly the tears she'd been fighting to hold back broke through and spilled down her face and her voice quivered as she said, "What do you know about anything, about what I want?" Her voice broke on a sob. "Oh, Shane, please give me a chance!"

He uttered a strangled sound as he reached out and pulled her down to lie against him. "Don't, Karen. Oh, sweetheart, don't cry. I can't stand it!"

Her sobs continued unrestrained as she snuggled into his arms, and his hands caressed her. Finally she spoke into his shoulder. "I know you don't want me but I have to be here. I'd go crazy back at the house wondering how you are, if you were being well cared for."

His lips teased her hair. "Don't want you? You know better than that. After all, there's no way I can hide how much I want you."

He molded her to the contours of his body, only the bedclothes between them.

She tipped her head back and looked at him. "Then why?"

He guided her head back to his shoulder and said, "Because I'd finally steeled myself to leave you and every mile I put between us was like a knife twisted in my guts. I rammed the car into that tree because I was literally blind with grief and didn't see the curve." She gasped but he continued. "I knew if I gave in to my need for you and asked you to come I wouldn't have the strength to send you away again."

She smiled and nuzzled her parted lips in the hollow of his throat causing him to shiver with pleasure. "I'm glad because I don't intend to be sent away. Not until we've fulfilled the purpose of this marriage, which, in case you've forgotten, is to have a baby."

"I haven't forgotten," he murmured, "but just because I want you more than I've ever wanted any other woman doesn't alter the fact that it won't last. I'm neither capable of nor interested in a long-lasting relationship with any one woman, and you are no exception. By the time you have conceived and borne a child I will be anxious to terminate the marriage. That was our agreement and it stands. I'll give you financial security in abundance, but that's all. Are you sure you understand?"

Karen would have agreed to anything. She'd

nearly lost him twice today, first when he walked out on her, and then in the automobile accident. Now all she wanted was to stay as close to him as she could get for as long as he would allow.

She could hear his heart hammering under her ear and she moved herself up until her face was level with his on the pillow. She cupped his cheeks in her hands and covered his mouth with her own. His arms tightened around her and he held the back of her head with his hand so she couldn't pull away as his response told her more eloquently than words ever could of his desire for her. Her fingers probed the edges of the bandage as she whispered against his mouth. "I understand, Shane. I promise not to make demands."

He buried his face in the scented softness of her neck and murmured, "I'm glad you came. If you hadn't I would have sent for you in spite of all my good intentions. I couldn't have helped myself. Oh Karen, I want you so much!"

She held him and stroked his bandaged head as his words flooded her with a quiet joy. He couldn't leave her any more than she could leave him. There was a bond between them that was too strong to be denied.

She caressed his dark hair with her lips as she asked, "How badly are you hurt? Is it serious?"

"They say I have a mild concussion but except for a monstrous headache and a tendency to be violently sick every so often I'm fine."

"Some fine," she grumbled as their lips met again. His mouth clung to hers with hungry insistence and they were both so engrossed in the kiss that neither of them heard the door open until a squeal from behind got their attention.

A heavyset middle-aged nurse stood by the door, her face stiff with disapproval. There was a suggestion of outrage in her voice as she said, "Really, Mr. McKittrick, we can't allow this type of thing." Her eyes shifted to Karen. "You'll have to get off the bed, miss. I'm afraid I'll have to ask you to leave; Mr. McKittrick is not supposed to have visitors."

Karen started to move away but Shane held her close as he said, "The lady is my wife and she's staying right here."

The nurse looked startled as she muttered, "Oh, well, she can remain but she'll have to stay off the bed; it's against hospital rules."

"I'm not interested in hospital rules!" Shane's temper was rising fast. "Now get out of here; we'll push the call button if we need you!"

The nurse pulled herself up to her full height and said, "Well!" then turned and stalked out of the room.

Shane sank back against the pillow as though the brief spurt of anger had drained him of all strength. Karen could see the pounding pulse in his temple and knew he must be in agony. She caressed his face gently with her fingertips and kissed his closed eyelids as she whispered, "Is there anything I can do to make you more comfortable?"

He kissed her finger as it slid across his mouth. "You're already doing it. Who taught you those subtle little ways of pleasing a man?"

She smiled. "No one. I just do what comes naturally and you seem to like it."

"*Seem* to like it?" He took her hand and held it against the pain in his head. "That's a masterpiece of understatement! You wind me around those tiny fingers of yours and you know it."

Oh, how she wished that were true! If she could only tell him how much she loved him. She gently soothed his aching head with her fingers and could feel him relaxing into sleep when the door opened again and a man walked in followed by the same nurse who had interrupted them earlier. Shane opened his eyes and groaned with the effort of turning his head. The man looked at Shane then at Karen perched on the bed beside him and said, "I'm Dr. Flemming, Mr. McKittrick. I treated you when you were brought in, remember?"

Shane murmured, "Vaguely."

The doctor cleared his throat. "It's against the hospital rules for Mrs. McKittrick to be on the bed with you."

Shane took Karen's hand and squeezed it. "So I understand."

The doctor looked embarrassed. "Well, look, I can understand your wanting her with you, but you really will rest better if she'll leave and come back tomorrow."

"The hell I will! If she leaves I'm going with her."

"Oh, now, Mr. McKittrick we can't possibly allow that!" He sounded thoroughly alarmed. "It may be several days before you're well enough to be discharged."

Shane looked at Karen. "How did you get here?"

She said, "I drove the Corvette. But, Shane, be sensible—"

"I am being sensible. I want you to take me home."

The doctor sputtered as Karen replied. "Shane, you'd never stand the trip. Wait until you're feeling better tomorrow—"

Shane sat up and held his head in both hands as if afraid it would blow apart. Karen put her arms around him and held him against her as she continued to soothe him.

"The doctor's right; a concussion is nothing to fool around with. You're in so much pain you can hardly move. They'll give you something to make you sleep and I'll be right here. I'll sit in a chair by the bed and hold your hand. Dr. Flemming will let me stay, won't you, doctor?"

She glared at the confused man and he spoke quickly. "Of course."

Shane straightened up and lowered his legs over the side of the bed and began unfastening the hospital gown he was wearing.

"I'm going home," he said stubbornly. "Karen, go down to the business office and make arrangements for me to leave and, doctor, get that woman"—he nodded to the nurse—"out of here and send someone in to help me dress."

The trip home was a nightmare. Karen's nerves were stretched taut as she guided the powerful car through the misty, shifting fog along the coast. Shane was slumped in the other seat, his face gray with pain and nausea, and he was shivering with cold. She should never have allowed him to talk her into this folly! She should have insisted he stay in the hospital, but she'd never been able to deny him anything, except on their wedding night. She shuddered at the memory of that awful night, thinking that

her fears then were nothing compared to the fear she was feeling now. She should l v°
refused to bring him home, made him stay in the hospital, but she'd wanted him with her so badly. He'd said he needed her and she wanted to take care of him.

Karen turned into the driveway and stopped the car as close as she could to the front door Mrs. Whitney appeared almost immediately and opened Shane's door. She had lost her usual calm and looked worried and upset. She told him how relieved she was that he wasn't seriously injured as she helped him out of the car. Mrs. Whitney was a tall woman, and strong, and she was able to support his height and weight where Karen could not. Together they got him upstairs and sat him on the edge of the bed; Karen removed his shirt and shoes and helped him into his long velour robe. Mrs. Whitney turned up the heat on Shane's side of the electric blanket and left.

Karen unbuckled his belt and said, "Can you stand so I can pull off your slacks?"

He managed a weak grin. "I'll stand anytime you want to take off my pants, sweetheart."

She blushed and helped him to his feet.

She left on his briefs and again wrapped the heavy robe around him, then helped him into bed and pulled up the blankets. He was still shivering, but not quite so violently, and she turned off the bedside light as she said, "Close your eyes and relax. I'll be back in a minute."

Actually it was five minutes before she came back, dressed in a mint green cloud of chiffon that was one of her trousseau nighties, and crawled into bed beside him. Shane turned toward her and she reached for him and cradled his head against the softness of her breasts. He drew her close and buried his face against her as he murmured. "Oh Karen, sweet Karen, you're so soft."

She lightly massaged the tight muscles at the nape of his neck. "How does this feel, Shane? Does it help?"

He groaned. "Do you need to ask? I wonder, though, if later you'll ever be able to forgive me."

"Forgive you for what?"

He kissed her partially exposed breast. "For making such a failure of my noble plans for sending you away."

She smiled in the dark. "Go to sleep, darling. We don't have to worry about that now."

Karen woke to the sound of water splashing in the bathroom. It was still dark but a suggestion of light was beginning to show at the closed drapes. A shaft of brilliance made a path through the darkness before the bathroom light was flicked off and she heard Shane making his way across the room. He climbed into bed beside her and she murmured sleepily, "Shane, are you all right?"

"I'm fine. I didn't mean to wake you." He took her in his arms and pressed her against him. She stiffled a gasp as she realized that he was completely naked. His body was long and lean and muscular. She tried to combat her tenseness as she said, "Does your head still hurt?"

His lips caressed her face. "Yes, but it's more bearable now."

He nuzzled the hollow of her neck below her

ear and sent tingles in all directions. She relaxed in his arms.

He raised his head and his lips teased hers, then moved down her slender throat as he pushed aside her deeply cut nightgown. She gasped with pleasure and wound her fingers in his dark hair.

Her nightie was tossed to the floor and his exploring hands sent tongues of fire through her. She arched her body against his and her voice quivered as she said, "Tell me what you want me to do, Shane."

"You're doing just fine. We'll take it slowly; I don't want to frighten you again."

He did take it slowly until finally it was Karen who begged for release, and when it came she lost all hold on reality and soared. When she finally touched earth again she lay snuggled in Shane's arms, satiated and content. She tugged at his ear lobe with her teeth and whispered, "Oh, Shane. I love you so."

His smile slowly died and a fleeting look of pain swept across his face as he said, "No, Karen, it's not love you feel for me. I've just introduced you into the mystery and joy of passion, and it's easy to confuse that with love. Don't make that mistake, Karen. I don't want to hurt you."

She shuddered as his remark hit home and vowed to be more careful in the future. Shane didn't want love from her and she'd have to keep her feelings for him under stricter control. She mustn't let him know how deeply she cared.

He must have realized how his words had hurt because he lifted her face and kissed her. "For a beginner, Mrs. McKittrick, you were slightly spectacular. It's a good thing I've got this pounding headache. I'd never have been able to be as gentle with you if I'd felt even halfway decent."

Oh, no, she'd forgotten about his concussion! She gasped and put her hand to the hammering pulse at his temple as she said, "I'm sorry, Shane, I forgot. We should have waited.

He groaned as he gathered her to him. "No way! I'd waited as long as I could. There's a limit to any man's endurance and mine had been reached, believe me! The pain of wanting you was a great deal worse than the pain in my head."

The next three weeks were pure heaven, or would have been if Karen had been able to forget that hers wasn't a normal marriage, that her husband was humoring her only until he got the one thing he wanted—a son. They took trips to Lake Tahoe, to Disneyland, where Karen was wide-eyed with delight, and to San Francisco for the opera—but always their nights were spent making love and Karen was a little embarrassed to admit that she liked that best of all. Shane tried to be gentle but more often than not their hunger for each other could not be controlled and their loving was violent and immensely satisfying.

Then came the day when Karen knew she was not yet pregnant. She shuddered at the thought of telling Shane. He asked only one thing of her, a child, and in spite of all their loving she had failed him. Would he be angry and blame her? She didn't think she could stand it if he withdrew again and treated her like a little girl who could never do anything right.

Karen was sitting hunched over on the side of

the bed when Taffy came in bearing a tray with a coffeepot and two cups. She beamed a greeting as she said, "Good morning, sleepyhead. Your husband sent me up to have a cup of coffee with you and to tell you he had to go in to Carmel for a while but will be back for lunch."

She set the tray on the round table and turned to look at Karen. What she saw made her frown. "Honey, are you sick?"

Karen shook her head. "Not really; I think I'll just go back to sleep for a while."

Karen tossed restlessly, neither asleep or awake, and her dreams were disjointed and frightening. Something—a noise, perhaps— made her jump and open her eyes. The heavy drapes were still pulled across the French doors and the room was dim. There was another noise, which she identified as a footstep, and the door opened. Shane walked in, his mouth set in a thin line. He walked to the bed and stood looking down at her as he said, "Taffy said you were still in bed. What's the matter? Don't you feel well?"

She was caught and she hadn't had a chance to plan a way to break her news to him easily. She looked up at him through thick dark lashes and stammered, "I—I'm all right—my—my stomach hurts."

He sat down on the side of the bed and put his hand to her forehead. "Did you eat something that didn't agree with you? You don't seem to be running a temperature."

She shook her head. "No, Shane, I'm trying to tell you I'm not pregnant. In spite of all our lovemaking I'm not going to give you a child."

The tears she'd been fighting to hold back spilled over and ran down her cheeks as with a muttered oath Shane took her in his arms and held her close.

"Karen, is that what's upsetting you so? Didn't you ever have sex education in school? It sometimes takes months to get pregnant—even years—and you're so very young. Don't be in such a hurry; think of all the fun we can have trying."

She couldn't believe what she was hearing. He sounded almost glad she wasn't pregnant! But that wasn't possible—he was anxious for an heir! She hiccuped on a sob and said, "But you said you expected a baby within a year! You know I should be pregnant by now!"

He swore quietly and stroked her tousled hair. "Let's just forget it, okay?"

Her green eyes sought and held his brown ones as she asked, "Are you sure?"

He kissed her then, tenderly, almost lovingly. "Of course I'm sure. Now, do you want me to have Mrs. Whitney serve lunch up here?"

She smiled mistily. "No, I feel better. I'll dress and go downstairs."

Karen and Shane spent some of their time in San Francisco, where they became part of the social scene and Shane could catch up on what work he couldn't have transferred to his home on the Monterey Peninsula. His sophisticated friends were intrigued by his child bride and Shane seemed to enjoy showing her off, although he was possessive and let everyone know it. It was in San Francisco that they also came in contact with Audrey again.

Shane came back to the condominium one afternoon with the news that Audrey had returned from her round-the-world tour and that they were invited to a welcome home party for her the following night. That was one party Karen did not want to attend, but she smilingly agreed and asked, "Does Audrey know we're married?"

He nodded. "Oh, yes, news travels fast. She said to give you her best wishes."

A little shock ran through Karen as she said, "You've talked to her?"

"Mm-hm—she stopped by the office this morning to offer her congratulations."

Karen felt a sharp twinge of jealousy. What had Shane and Audrey's relationship been? She was almost sure they'd been lovers; Audrey's attitude toward him left little doubt on that score. How had she taken the news of his marriage to Karen? Karen was sure that Audrey wasn't the type to accept defeat gracefully.

Karen was right. Audrey was the center of attention at the party given by one of the state's most powerful political figures at his mansion atop Nob Hill. Audrey looked stunning in a classically cut gown in a creamy jersey that draped around her slender height and accentuated the russet highlights in her soft mahogany hair.

She must have been watching for Shane because as soon as he and Karen were ushered into the room she practically threw herself into his arms and kissed him full on the mouth. Shane broke away and laughed as he said, "Behave yourself, Audrey."

"Well, really, darling"—she pouted—"we're not going to stop being friends just because you're married to little Karen are we?" Her turquoise eyes were chips of ice as they raked over Karen. "Hello, Karen, you're looking sweet tonight. Like the kitten that just caught the canary. You should be careful pet, some things are quite indigestible."

Karen shivered as Shane put his arm around her waist and frowned, but Audrey was gone as quickly as she had appeared. She was charming for the rest of the evening but Karen was uneasy. Audrey was a threat and one Karen had no defense against.

They returned to Carmel the following day and left the shadow of Audrey behind—or almost. Karen's love for Shane was all-encompassing. It radiated from her arms when she held him, her lips when she kissed him, and her body when it was entwined with his in lovemaking, but she was uneasily aware that it was not the same with him. He was passionate, and tender, and more than a little possessive. He gave her anything she wanted and spoiled her outrageously, but sometimes, early in the morning, before daylight, she would wake to find him standing at the window or just sitting in the leather armchair staring ahead at nothing, a sad, brooding look on his unguarded face.

The first time it happened she was alarmed and sat up in bed, sleepy and disoriented, as she said, "Shane, is something wrong? Why are you up so early?"

She could have sworn that for just a second the look he turned on her was one of annoyance, but then he smiled and held out his arms and she crawled out of bed and onto his lap and he cuddled her as he said, "Nothing's wrong; I'm sorry I disturbed you with my restlessness."

He stroked her and kissed her and very shortly carried her back to bed, but the next time it happened, and the next, and the next, she pretended to sleep so she could watch him. Sometimes he sat or stood quietly, other times he paced silently around the room, and once he dressed quickly and left, returning more than an hour later.

During these times Karen lay shivering between the warm sheets, apprehensive and afraid. Was Shane tiring of her already? Was he longing for Audrey with her more experienced and exotic lovemaking? Karen knew what a novice she was in the art of love. Maybe Shane was bored with her innocence. Was he already regretting the desire that had trapped him into this marriage with a girl who was little more than a child?

Her fears were forgotten each time he returned to bed and reached for her, but they returned at unexpected moments and left her troubled and uneasy.

Then nature finally cooperated and one day Karen realized, as a little thrill ran through her, that she was going to have Shane's child. Shane's son. Was it really possible? Shane was driving to San Francisco for the day later in the week. She'd ride up with him and see Dr. Karl Laird, one of the city's leading obstetricians and a longtime friend of Shane's. She said nothing about her appointment to Shane, however. She wanted to wait until she was sure.

Karl Laird was about Shane's age. She'd met him before and liked him. He teased her about not wasting any time, then examined her and took blood for tests. He told her to go shopping for a couple of hours and then come back. She nervously left and when she returned the nurse ushered her right into the doctor's office. He was sitting behind his desk grinning and Karen sank down in the chair opposite, her knees suddenly weak.

Karl said, "Congratulate your husband for me, Karen; he'll be a father by next July.

The beginnings of a smile played around Karen's mouth as she said, "Really? Are you sure?"

Karl leaned back in his chair. "It's a little early to be positive but I'd bet my reputation on it."

The smile broke into full radiance. "Oh, Karl, thank you!"

He laughed. "Don't thank me, honey, I had nothing to do with it." She blushed and he was suddenly serious. "I've never thought of Shane as the father type. Is he going to be surprised about this?"

"Oh, no," Karen beamed, "we planned this baby. It's very much wanted."

Karl relaxed and smiled. "Great! You're in excellent health and shouldn't have any problems. Come back in a month and bring Shane if he wants to come. I know he'll have questions."

Karen was bursting with excitement as she sat beside Shane on the ride to Carmel but she didn't want to tell him her secret yet. It was special news and should be told in a special setting. She'd wait until they were in bed, after they'd made love, when they were warm and relaxed and loving. Then she'd tell him that she'd finally done something right—that she'd conceived the child that meant so much to him, the child he'd married her to get. She pushed the unpleasant thought aside and shivered with anticipation. Shane glanced at her and put his hand on her knee as he asked, "Are you cold, honey?"

She hugged his arm and shook her head. "No, I'm just happy."

His fingers tightened around her knee and his face softened and he leaned over and kissed the top of her head. "You're the easiest woman to please that I ever met. What's made you so happy now?"

Embarrassed, and afraid that he would read her secret in her eyes, she turned away.

Henri had dinner ready when they got home and afterward they curled up together in the big leather chair in the den, watching television until Shane carried her upstairs to bed.

Later, as they lay warm and tousled and a little breathless, Karen knew the time had come to share her secret. She started hesitantly as she snuggled in his arms.

"Shane, are you happy?"

His hand rested across her midriff as he murmured sleepily, "Mmmm, I'm estatic. Nothing in the world could make me happier than I am at this minute."

"Nothing?"

"Nothing!"

She was going to have to be a bit more specific. "Don't you remember why you married me?"

His teeth worried her ear lobe. "Of course I do. I married you because I couldn't keep my hands off you."

She giggled and reached over to turn on the

bedside lamp. She wanted to see his face when she told him. She tried again.

"You're not being serious and I have something very important to tell you."

He grinned and kissed her nose. "All right, Karen, what is it? Are you overdrawn at the bank? Or did you charge something wildly expensive to my account? Either way I promise not to beat you."

"I'm pregnant!" she blurted, unable to hold it in any longer.

His reaction was totally different from what she had expected. He stiffened and stared at her as the blood drained from his face. Finally he said, "Are you sure?"

She smiled tentatively and nodded. "I saw Dr. Laird this morning and he did a blood test. He says it's almost certain."

"Almost?" Shane watched her closely. "Then he could be mistaken?"

Karen felt cold with shock. What was the matter with him? She'd thought he'd be wild with joy and he acted almost disappointed! Maybe he was just being cautious, afraid it might be a mistake after all. She shook her head.

"Darling, it's highly unlikely that the test is wrong. They're very accurate and it isn't as if we hadn't been trying to have a baby." She grinned impishly. "I don't see how I could *not* be pregnant."

He swung back the covers and sat on the edge of the bed. He sounded angry as he muttered.

"Why did you have to be so damned eager? Are you anxious to have this baby so you can leave me?"

"Shane!" Karen sat up too and reached for her

yellow robe. "I don't understand! I thought you'd
be so happy!"

She slipped on the robe and sat with brimming
eyes and trembling lips, attempting not to shiver
as she tried again to understand. "You're the one
who wanted a baby—why are you so angry?"

Shane looked at her with a little groan and
took her in his arms, rocking her back and forth.
"I'm not angry, sweetheart, I'm just shocked.
I—I thought it would take longer. I'm sorry. Of
course I'm happy, but I'm worried, too. Are you
all right? What did Karl Laird say?"

Karen held back the tears and relaxed a little.
Maybe he *hadn't* expected her to get pregnant
quite so soon. Maybe he *was* worried about her.
But when they lay down again he kissed her
lightly and turned away from her, and for the
first time since their marriage had really begun
they didn't sleep in each other's arms.

For the next two weeks Shane made love to
her only occasionally, and almost reluctantly,
as though he would rather not but couldn't help
himself. Karen was puzzled and upset and when
she questioned him he explained that he didn't
want to overtire her or endanger the child. She
tried to tell him that Dr. Laird had said it was
perfectly all right to make love, but then one
morning she leaped out of bed and ran to the
bathroom, where she was violently sick. Shane
immediately moved her back into the lavender
bedroom, where she once again slept alone. He
was patient and loving and told her she would
sleep better if she had her own room, but she felt
bewildered and deserted and remembered, too
late, that he hadn't wanted a wife—only a
woman who would give him a son! The days of

Karen's marriage were drawing to a close. Once
Shane's son was born he would have no further
need of her—he'd made that very clear. By July
she would be a free woman again. Free. She
considered the word. How ironic that she would
never be free again, but that, in fact, the divorce
would leave her more Shane's prisoner than
ever.

Chapter Eight

Karen's pregnancy was not an easy one; her nausea continued unabated and, instead of disappearing as the day progressed, lasted all day. She lost weight and the circles that had appeared under her eyes deepened daily.

One morning, she crawled back into bed after a particularly violent session only to hear Shane enter the room behind her. He stood angrily over her bed and spoke.

"I'll send Taffy up to help you dress, then I'm taking you back to San Francisco to see Dr. Laird." She started to protest but he paid no attention. "I'm not stupid, Karen, and I know most women don't suffer the way you are. Now don't argue. I'll be ready to go as soon as you are dressed."

Shane must have called ahead because they were ushered into Dr. Laird's private office as soon as they arrived. Karl came in a few minutes later, looking worried, and said, "What's the problem? Shane says you're having a rough time with nausea. You should have contacted me sooner; I can give you shots to relieve that."

Shane looked straight at the doctor and said, "Karl, I want this pregnancy terminated."

Karl frowned. "Karen said you wanted a baby."

Shane stood and began to pace. "I did, but not at the expense of her health. She's too young. We can have a baby later, when she's older."

Karen stared. What was the matter with Karl? Why wasn't he laughing, joking, reminding Shane that it was a little late to change his mind? But he didn't. He was serious as he said, "I'll examine Karen again, of course, but she was in excellent health when I saw her three weeks ago. The decision to abort has to be Karen's, Shane. You can't force her into it."

Abort! Oh, no, Shane wanted her to have an abortion! It hadn't even occurred to her that *that* was what he was talking about. She jumped up and a wave of dizziness swept over her as she screamed, *"No!* Shane, how could you!"

The dizziness increased and she sank back into the chair. Shane squatted down on his heels beside her and took her hand in his. The lines around his mouth deepened as he said, "Karen, I'm worried about you. You don't just suffer from morning sickness—it never lets up. You can't keep anything down and you've lost nearly ten pounds."

Karen shook her head, still weak with shock. "It's only temporary, Shane, and you heard Karl—there are shots that will help."

The desperation in Shane's eyes deepened. "Damn it, honey, if you won't think of yourself, think of the baby! If you can't eat you can't nourish it. It may be born with brain damage, or worse."

Karen's eyes widened. It wasn't shock she was feeling now, it was horror! He wasn't concerned about her—it was the baby he was worried about. The baby might be damaged and that would be totally unacceptable to him! His son, the heir to his precious business, could never be less than perfect! She tore her hand from his and cringed against the side of the chair.

"I hate you!" she spat. "You can't stand the thought that your child might be flawed! Rather than face that you want to throw it away and start over with a woman who has the good sense to have an easy pregnancy!"

He stared at her, his face gray. "Karen, it's not like that!"

Suddenly, all the fight went out of her. How could she ever hope to win against a man like Shane? Numbly, she allowed herself to be led into Dr. Laird's immaculate examining room. She hardly noticed as the doctor sternly told Shane to leave before he made things any worse, but she *was* surprised to see Shane obey. She had never been able to tell him anything, and she was his wife! She supposed that this was just one more item that proved that she should never have entered his life in the first place.

An hour later, Karen had been examined. Dr. Laird gave her a shot to calm the nausea and a bottle of capsules to keep it under control, then took Shane into his office for a private conversation.

Karen lay on the table feeling numb and lethargic. Probably a result of the tranquilizer, she thought, but she didn't like the feeling of detachment. She wanted to be in control of her emotions, not floating off somewhere on a cloud.

Besides, it didn't do a thing to relieve the anguish that was tearing her apart. How could she have been so wrong about Shane? She'd been attracted to him right from the beginning in spite of his overbearing manner and his tendency to control everyone around him. She'd been so sure that under that brusque, businesslike exterior there was a sensitive, compassionate man who was capable of love in spite of his determination not to feel it. Love! He didn't know the meaning of the word! He didn't have a heart, he had a computer, and there was no place in either his life or his business for a son who might have a weakness—who might just be human!

The nurse came in to help Karen dress and a few minutes later Shane and the doctor came back. Shane put his arm around her waist, but she moved away and walked out of the office. On the way back to the condominium Shane tried to talk to her, but she sat, quiet and unmoving, on her own side of the car until he gave up. When they got back to the apartment he carried her small travel case into the master bedroom. Two hours ago she would have been wildly happy, but now she merely paused in the doorway and said, "I'll be using the guest room, Shane; take my case in there."

They stayed in San Francisco for five days until they were sure the pills would keep the nausea under control. They did. Karen was no longer sick, but she ate only because Shane insisted. Her appetite was nonexistent. So was her enthusiasm for life. She spoke only when spoken to, slept when she was told to go to bed, and the rest of the time she curled up in front of the television set with a book in her lap but looked at neither of them. She felt disembodied, detached from herself, like a spectator aware of what was going on but taking no part in it.

Shane looked pale and drawn. He talked to her, trying vainly to interest her in something, anything, but although she listened carefully she made no effort to keep up her end of the conversation. Finally he asked her if she'd like to go home to Carmel. The idea appealed to her. She loved the house on the side of the cliff overlooking the wide, cool Pacific.

They went home and Karen was happier. She had Taffy, who didn't know the meaning of depression. Shane had apparently asked Taffy for help because she coaxed Karen to eat, took her for walks, and insisted they go shopping in Carmel. Gradually Karen began to emerge from the shocklike state that had kept her prisoner. She could talk with Taffy about everything but her problems with Shane.

Then Mark arrived.

Mark was the only person who knew the truth about Shane and Karen's marriage and he was the only one she could discuss it with, but she'd had no time alone with Mark since her wedding day. She suspected that he was avoiding her, not so much because of his disapproval of their arrangement as because he knew how possessive Shane was toward her and didn't want to incur his wrath.

One day, two weeks after the scene in the doctor's office, Mark arrived at the house with a briefcase full of important business papers and spent the day closeted with Shane in the office. At dinner that evening his conversation was directed mainly at Karen and was put in such a way that she would have been rude if she hadn't responded. The talk centered around general topics and she began to forget her depression as her interest was captured. After desert, however, she excused herself and went into the library.

The library was her favorite room and she'd spent a lot of time there lately. It was the room that had brought her to Shane's magnificent home on the Monterey Peninsula and for a while she'd been happy there. She didn't have the energy or the interest to continue her cataloguing, but she loved to sit on the red velour sofa and look at the row upon row of handsomely bound books. She didn't feel quite so lonely there.

She'd been sitting there only a few minutes when the door opened and Mark entered and shut it behind him. He was alone and didn't wait to be asked before sitting down on the couch beside her. He had a tall drink in each hand and offered her one as he took a sip of the other. She took hers and sank back against the cushions but said nothing. Mark spoke first.

"Karen, I want to know what's going on here. You've lost all your sparkle. You only go through the motions of being alive and Shane looks like he's been dragged through the desert."

Karen shrugged. "I'm sorry Shane has to suffer. He's afraid the baby will be damaged because of my illness and he wants no part of an imperfect child."

Mark stared at her then exploded. "Where on earth did you get an idea like that?"

She answered with another question. "Do you know he wanted me to have an abortion?" She didn't dare add what she thought to herself: And still does.

Mark nodded. "I know he suggested it—" Karen started to interrupt and he hurried on, "All right, I suppose he *demanded* it, but you know Shane, honey. He's used to issuing orders and having them obeyed and he was desperately concerned for you!"

She set her glass on the coffee table. "Has he been discussing this with you?"

"Yes, he has," Mark confessed. "He'll do anything to pull you out of this lethargy you're mired in—even confide in me—and that was quite a concession because he knows how I feel about you."

She shifted uncomfortably. "Please, Mark—"

He held up a hand for silence. "Don't worry, I'm not here on my own behalf. Karen, you know I did everything I could to keep you from marrying Shane. I told you it would take someone tougher and more mature than you to weather a marriage based on Shane's idiotic proposal, and you've proved me right. At the first sign of trouble you fall completely apart."

Karen drew a sharp breath of protest but Mark continued. "I'll admit Shane needs to be taken down a peg once in a while but, honey, do you have to torture him?"

It had been weeks since Karen had felt any emotion but now it was pure outrage that coursed through her. The nerve of him suggesting that *she* was at fault when it was Shane who wanted to get rid of the baby! She drew herself up and exploded in righteous indignation.

"*Me* torture *him*? I should have known you

wouldn't understand! Do you want me to have an abortion just so he can have peace of mind?"

The brief outburst over, she slumped against the cushions. "If Shane loved me I could understand and even be flattered that he preferred me to the baby, but he doesn't care about me. All he cares about is providing a fine healthy specimen of manhood to carry on his wonderful business."

Mark snorted with frustration. "Karen, how can you be so obtuse? Of course Shane loves you! Oh, he won't admit it, even to himself, but no woman can torment a man the way you're tormenting Shane if he doesn't love her, want her, need her. Grow up, little girl, and stop giving Shane good reason to be afraid to love you!"

He slammed his glass down on the coffee table as he turned and stalked out of the room.

Karen didn't join Shane and Mark in the den but went upstairs to bed. Mark's taunts had cut through the fog of bitterness that had enveloped her lately and hit their mark. Why did she go on loving Shane when she knew what a monster he was? But was he really as bad as she pictured him? He'd always been concerned about her—in fact, it was his concern for her after her house burned down that had caused him to agree to marry her, so why did she find it impossible to believe it was his concern for her that made him want her to have an abortion?

She rolled to the other side of the bed and punched the pillow, trying to get comfortable. A door opened and closed and she knew it was Shane coming into the bedroom next door. She pictured him as he had been at dinner, dressed in gray slacks and a navy blue blazer. For the first time she realized that his shoulders had slumped wearily and he had only picked at his food. He was losing weight and she could see what she hadn't noticed before: his face was drawn and haggard and there were deep circles under his eyes.

She heard him in the bathroom running water, brushing his teeth. Was he really suffering as Mark said? She'd been so sunk in her own misery she hadn't even noticed how he was feeling.

She sat up and turned on the bedside light. The hands on the clock radio pointed to midnight. She'd been wrestling with her feelings for Shane for over two hours. They couldn't go on like this; they had to get things straightened out before they both came unglued. She slid out of bed and walked, barefoot and wearing only a sleeveless, low-cut nightgown, through the bathroom and into Shane's room.

The room was dark but the light from her room provided enough illumination for her to find her way around without stumbling. There was a movement on the bed and Shane's voice called, "Is that you, Karen?"

She walked to the bed and stood looking down at him. "Yes, Shane, can we talk?"

It was too dark to see his expression, but he propped himself up on his elbow and said, "That's all I've wanted the past two weeks—just a chance to sit down with you and talk."

She sat on the side of the bed. "Why do you want to get rid of our baby?"

She heard his sharp intake of breath but he didn't move. "I don't, now that you're no longer sick, but it tore me apart to stand by while you lost weight you didn't have to spare. I had no intention of standing by and letting you ruin your health just to give me a child."

Karen shivered and realized that she was cold as she rubbed her bare arms with her hands. Shane threw back the covers and said, "You'd better get under the blanket—you mustn't catch cold."

She crawled into his big bed and snuggled down under the silken sheet and heavy blanket, but he made no move to touch her. Her green eyes studied the face she could see only dimly.

Then he brushed a strand of hair away from her face and his voice broke as he said, "Don't torture me anymore, Karen. I don't think I can stand it!"

With a little cry she wound her arms around his neck and pulled him down to her.

The next two months were a continuation of their interrupted honeymoon. They gave several small parties and were entertained in return. The only flaw in Karen's happiness was the presence of Audrey, who showed up at all the gatherings. She was always overly friendly toward Shane but never got out of line. There was nothing definite Karen could complain about but somehow Audrey always made her feel like a teenager making a fool of herself around the grown-ups. When Karen's child got large enough to round out her figure it was always Audrey who made caustic little remarks like, "Karen, are you sure you're not gaining weight too fast?" or "Really, dear, you shouldn't pour yourself into jeans now that your tummy is protruding so."

Shane, however, was frankly delighted by the new fullnes of her breasts and the roundness of her derriere, and he handled her gently but with passion. When the need became apparent he sent her back to the couturier who had supplied her trousseau and had custom-designed maternity clothes made for her.

Karen was so happy it seemed almost too good to last. It was.

She was six months pregnant in April when the first rift appeared in the person of a Mr. Homer Green, who called one day when Shane was out and said he had urgent business and must see Shane as soon as possible. Karen gave him an appointment for the following morning. Shane was as mystified as she was when she told him of the call.

Mr. Green appeared promptly the next morning. He was a short, bald, well-dressed man, who introduced himself as an attorney from a well-known law firm in San Francisco. He assured them that his business concerned both Mr. and Mrs. McKittrick, since it was a family matter. They went into the office and Mr. Green got right to the point.

"Mr. McKittrick, it's my unpleasant duty to inform you that your mother, Katherine McKitrick Durrell, died of a cerebral hemorrhage two weeks ago in Orléans, France."

Karen gasped and felt Shane stiffen beside her, but his voice was cold as he said, "What has this to do with me?"

Mr. Green didn't seem surprised as he answered, "I understand you had been estranged for some time. However, she left you a substantial inheritance, which I have been instructed to turn over to you." He reached into his expensive leather briefcase and withdrew some legal-looking papers.

Shane's face was stony. "I gather she had remarried?"

Mr. Green nodded. "She was a widow. Monsieur Durrell died two years ago. He was an artist—quite well known in France, I understand. Part of your mother's estate is paintings, which I'm told will bring a handsome sum when sold."

Shane made a tight, jerky motion with his hands. "I don't want them. I don't want anything from her!"

"Shane, darling." Karen moved closer to Shane on the couch and put her arm through his. "This has upset you. Maybe Mr. Green can come back tomorrow."

Shane glanced down at her and there was no warmth in the look. "Karen, it's not necessary for you to stay. Since I haven't seen my mother since before you were born, this can hardly concern you. Run along and I'll join you in a few minutes."

His dismissal hurt. She wanted to be with him, to ease the pain she knew he was feeling even if he wouldn't admit it. She rubbed her cheek against his arm and said, "But I want to stay."

He pulled away from her and stood. "I'd rather you left, Karen."

She had no choice but to bid Mr. Green goodbye and leave.

Shane and Mr. Green were closeted together

for nearly two hours. Karen took her daily walk around the estate and returned to the house just as Mr. Green was getting into his car.

Karen knocked on the door of Shane's office and went in. Shane was sitting behind the desk, looking off into space. She quickly crossed to him and put her arms around him, holding his head against her breast. He didn't protest but neither did he relax and enjoy her caresses as he usually did. She leaned down and kissed him as she said, "I'm sorry about your mother, Shane. Is there anyone who should be notified? Can I help?"

His arms circled her waist, but instead of answering her questions he said, "I've arranged for her estate to be liquidated and the money given to various charities."

She drew back in surprise. "But Shane—"

He jerked away angrily. "Oh, don't worry, I have plenty of money! You and the baby won't be deprived of anything!"

She blinked, unsure of what had brought on that outburst. "Shane!" I wasn't even thinking of such a thing! I just thought that if she wanted you to have the money—"

He turned back to his desk and riffled through some papers as he muttered, "I don't want to talk about it. I have work to do, Karen. Would you mind leaving me alone?"

With a quick movement and a few sharp words he had shut her out again and she felt numb with despair.

That night after they'd gone to bed Shane kissed her and turned away from her. It happened again the second night, and by the third day, Sunday, Karen was frantic. She couldn't stand his coldness and decided to try to find out what was wrong. After lunch she suggested that they go into the den, where they could talk.

It was Shane who took charge of the conversation, however. He set his coffee cup on the redwood burl table and said, "Your pregnancy seems to be progressing normally now, Karen. You haven't been sick for weeks and Karl Laird says you are healthy and carrying the baby well."

Karen smiled. "Yes, I feel fine. I told you there was no need to worry."

"Yes, well," Shane stood and walked over to the fireplace, "I find I can't run the business from here. I'm going to have to spend part of my time in San Francisco."

"That's all right—I don't mind living there part of the time," she said. "Maybe we can see some plays."

Shane frowned. "No, Karen, I'm not taking you with me. I want you settled in one place until the baby comes. I'll stay in the city Monday through Friday and come home on weekends, the way I did before."

She must have looked as stricken as she felt because he hurried on. "It will work out just fine. You'll have Taffy to keep you company and a house full of servants to see that things run smoothly. I'll call every day and come home on Friday afternoons. You'll hardly miss me."

Karen felt the life drain out of her. He was going to drive her out of her mind. Half the time he couldn't live without her and the other half he wanted nothing to do with her. What had caused this latest change of attitude? She wanted to scream, to throw something, but she didn't.

That night, however, it was she who turned away from him in the bed.

The following week was pure hell. Shane called once a day but there was no warmth in their conversation; it was a duty call to be sure she was all right. He wanted to be sure nothing happened to his precious child, she thought. She cried herself to sleep in the big lonely bed every night and wished she had never heard of Shane McKittrick.

Then on Thursday he told her he'd be home in time for dinner Friday evening, and the old excitement tingled through her. Shane was coming back! He would be home for two days and three nights! Certainly he couldn't ignore her all that time, not after the closeness that had, until so recently, existed between them?

Karen was waiting in the library when Shane's Cadillac, the car he'd bought to replace the Lincoln he'd wrapped around a tree, swung into the driveway. Her nerves were so taut that she would have heard him from anywhere in the house, but to make sure she had chosen to wait in the library, which was just off the entrance hall. She jumped up but made herself stay in the room. She wasn't going to run to him this time, he'd have to come to her.

She was standing by the desk when she heard him come in the front door. Her hands were clenched and her body was still with apprehension. How would he greet her? Would he come looking for her? Would he be happy to see her? Would he *want* her?

She was so intent on her agonizing that she didn't see him until he was standing in the door. Her eyes flew to his face and she felt herself relax. He looked pale and tired but the relief in his eyes was unmistakable. Without a word he held out his arms and she ran into them. Their lips and arms and bodies meshed and melted into one another as he murmured hoarsely, "Oh, Karen, how I missed you!"

They were thus occupied when a loud rap and an embarrassed cough sounded from the door. They both looked up guiltily to see Mrs. Whitney standing in the doorway, her flushed face turned discreetly away as she said, "Excuse me, I didn't mean—" She cleared her throat. "Dinner is ready to be served."

Dinner seemed interminable and when it was finally over Shane was in no mood for teasing. He took Karen by the hand and led her upstairs to bed.

They made love all weekend and Karen was content, but on Monday morning Shane left again for San Francisco. She was determined to make the best of this way of living if that's what Shane wanted, but she felt rejected, abandoned, and at last—used.

For the next three weeks he left on Monday morning and returned Friday afternoon, passionate and almost desperate in his need for her, but there was always something missing. The tender awareness that had always been a part of his relationship with her was gone, replaced by a hunger that she felt could be satisfied by almost any woman.

Their telephone conversations during the week became strained, then snappish, and by the fourth weekend the one thing she had thought could never happen did. She found it difficult to respond to his lovemaking; it was as

if his cold passion had finally destroyed her own
tender responses.

That Monday Shane took her back to San
Francisco with him because she had a Tuesday
appointment for her monthly checkup with Dr.
Laird. Karl weighed and probed and measured
and said she was coming along beautifully. She
complained that she was beginning to look like
an overinflated balloon, but he only laughed and
said that every woman felt that way and why
should she be any different?

It was late afternoon when she left the doctor's
office and took a cab back to the condominium.
She was anxious to be there when Shane got
home. Things were better between them here in
San Francisco. He seemed happy to have her
with him.

She changed out of her town clothes and into a
long, flowing caftan. Nothing could make her
look sexy now that she was over seven months
pregnant but the green delicately flowered material brought out the emerald color of her eyes
and heightened the rose in her cheeks. When the
doorbell rang she assumed it was Shane. Instead
it was Mark. He was carrying a briefcase and
smiled as he walked in.

"You're looking positively gorgeous, mama-
to-be. Where's the proud papa?"

Karen laughed. "He's not home yet. Come in
and have a drink—he should be here any minute."

They went into the living room and Mark
mixed a screwdriver for himself and handed
Karen a glass of orange juice. They sat together
on the gold damask couch and for a while the
conversation was general, but during a pause

Mark said quietly, "Karen, how's it going with you and Shane?"

She frowned and he hurried on. "You can tell me it's none of my business, but lately Shane's been hell to work for, and you're not looking too happy yourself. I feel responsible for getting you into this, honey, and I'd like to help you if you need it."

Karen toyed with her glass. Maybe she should confide in Mark. He was the only person she could talk to about her problems because only he knew the truth behind her marriage.

She started, cautiously at first, but when Mark listened carefully and offered no comment other than to take her hand when she began to get emotional, she forgot to be cautious and let the words flow. She poured out all her private anguish and without quite knowing how it happened she found herself in Mark's arms sobbing on his shoulder. They didn't hear the door open but Shane's voice boomed like thunder across the room. "What in hell is going on?"

They jerked apart guiltily and Karen cringed at the murderous look on Shane's face. He didn't move but his voice was chilling as he said, "I should have known! My sweet, naive, virginal wife can't wait until our baby's born to start cheating on me! And with one of the hired help!" He turned to Mark, his face livid. "I ought to kill you with my bare hands!"

He lunged at Mark, who jumped up and prepared to defend himself as Karen screamed, "Shane! Stop it! You're out of your mind!"

The hysteria in her voice must have gotten through to Shane because he stopped and jeered at her. "What's the matter? Are you afraid I'll mess up his pretty face? Well, you better believe I will!"

He started for Mark again. Karen instinctively stepped between them and before Shane could deflect the blow he had aimed at Mark it grazed Karen's shoulder, knocking her down.

The effect on Shane was instantaneous. He swore and dropped to the floor and gathered her in his arms as he groaned, "Sweetheart, are you all right? Oh, God, Karen, I'm sorry!"

Mark stood over them, his face twisted with rage. "You . . . You lay a hand on her again and I'll—"

Karen struggled to a sitting position and winced as pain shot through her right hip where she landed on it. This was the last straw! She'd had it with Shane and his moods, and with Mark, too! She pulled away from Shane and glared at him. "You have no right to accuse me of such a vile thing! I'm not your mother!"

Shane stiffened. "And just what is that supposed to mean?"

Karen held out her hand to Mark, who helped her off the floor. She was trembling with shock and anger as she said, "I know your mother ran off with another man and I'm sorry you were so hurt, but it doesn't give you the right to assume I'll behave the same way!"

Shane stood up and turned to Mark. "Get out of here, Mark, and don't ever let me catch you alone with my wife again!"

Mark glanced at Karen and left, slamming the door behind him.

Shane faced her and his voice was hoarse with surpressed violence as he said, "So, you've been listening to the servants' gossip! You should have pried a little further and gotten the whole story. My mother was a lot like you. Oh, not in looks—but she was just seventeen when she married Dad. He was thirty-seven, old enough to be her father, but he adored her. She was warm and innocent and loving and his whole life centered around her. I was born when she was twenty, and since there were no more children the three of us were very close. Until I was sent away to school when I was ten my mother was the most important person in my life. I loved her and was so proud when she came to school to visit me."

He turned and walked away, hunching his shoulders as if trying to escape the pain his memories ignited. "I was a freshman at an exclusive private boarding school when Mother disappeared. At first we thought she'd been kidnapped. Dad was a wealthy businessman and that type of thing was always a threat. All the law enforcement agencies were called in and it was two days before we found the note that had apparently dropped behind the bedside stand."

For a moment he was silent, and when he spoke again it was with an awful bitterness. "She'd gone away with an artist. A man her own age who was the current darling of the Carmel crowd. Of course the newspapers had a field day. By reporting her disappearance to the police as a suspected kidnapping, we gave the papers the perfect excuse for splashing our private agony all over their front pages."

Compassion overcame Karen's anger and she went to Shane and stood behind him, her arms around his waist and her cheek against his back.

"Darling, I know it was an awful experience but you can't let it distort your view of all women."

Shane didn't turn around or acknowledge her embrace and his voice was savage as he said, "You haven't the faintest idea what it was like so don't tell me how I should feel about women! You didn't see what her defection did to my father! He was like a man possessed. First he raged, then he cried, and finally he started to drink. I stayed home the rest of that school year, but I was only a kid—there was little I could do except be there when he needed to talk."

Shane moved away from her and started pacing the room. "It was hell! He'd start by calling her every vile name he could think of, then he'd sob and plead with her to come back, just as if she was in the room with us. I guess you could say he didn't handle his grief very well, but his whole life had blown up in his face!"

Shane stopped pacing and turned to Karen. The torment he was feeling was mirrored on his face but his voice was hard and cold. "I swore then that no woman would ever do that to me! If my mother, with her sweetness and innocence, couldn't be trusted, then there's no woman who can be. No, Karen, I have no reason to trust you. I need you only to give me a son—after that I shall expect you to get out of my life except where the child is concerned. And as long as you *are* my wife you will stay away from other men or I won't be responsible for what I might do!"

Chapter Nine

Karen felt sick. Shane's father wasn't the only one who'd had his life blow up in his face. It had just happened to her and she was stunned beyond belief.

Shane had told her from the beginning that he would not permit the marriage to extend beyond the birth of the baby, but she had been so sure she could change his mind, that he would fall in love with her and want her with him always. What a fool she'd been! What an idiot to think that a man as old and as experienced as Shane didn't know what he wanted.

Her legs were trembling and she sank down on the straight chair behind her. Well, she'd have to make the best of this impossible situation, but she didn't have to get in any deeper. She took a quivering breath and said, "I have no interest in other men, Shane, but since the objective of this marriage has been accomplished and I'm already pregnant there's no reason for us to sleep together anymore. There are less than two months left until the baby is born, then you'll be rid of me!"

Shane betrayed no emotion as he said, "As you like," and turned and walked out of the apartment.

They returned to Carmel and Karen again moved into the lavender room. She hated it. She hated Shane's mother and his father. She hated everyone but Shane. Why, oh why, couldn't she hate Shane? Maybe she was a masochist and got her kicks out of suffering? But then why was she so desperately unhappy?

Karen and Shane were coldly polite. They spent as little time as possible in each other's company and carried on lucid conversations about matters that had no depth. They both knew that they were only marking time until the baby was born and Karen could leave. Would Shane insist on seeing the baby often? She didn't think she could stand it if she had to continue this charade for eight years.

Shane took her back to San Francisco after two weeks for another checkup. Her due date was getting closer and her checkups more frequent. The doctor was a little concerned about the size of the baby, who was definitely bigger then average, but other than that she was doing fine.

That night Shane brought Audrey to the condominium for dinner. Audrey was tall and slender in a tight-fitting gown that showed off her luscious bosom and softly rounded hips. Karen felt like an overstuffed teddy bear and couldn't really blame Shane when his eyes kept straying to Audrey. Karen sat pushing food around on her plate and only half listening to Shane and Audrey discuss the worsening economic situation, but her attention was captured when Audrey said, "Would you mind if I dropped in on you at the house for a few days this week? I promised Paula—you remember Paula Jensen, darling, the one who paints all those ghastly seascapes—well, I promised to help her with her one-woman show in Carmel and hotel rooms always give me claustrophobia."

Shane smiled and said, "We'd love to have you, wouldn't we, Karen?"

Karen gave him a murderous glance and nodded.

So now they had Audrey as a houseguest. Not that she bothered Karen; Audrey hardly even spoke to *her*. All Audrey's attention was focused on Shane. They spent hours on the Pebble Beach golf course with their wealthy friends while Karen stayed home and fretted.

It was on the third night that Audrey was there that the nightmare began. Karen had been having trouble sleeping, not only because of her personal problems but because the baby filled her so completely that she couldn't get comfortable. The child was big and Karen was tiny and the combination was impossible. On this particular evening after dinner she had taken a couple of antacid pills and gone upstairs to lie down. She was always tired these days. Shane opened the door to her room a few minutes later and said, "Karen, are you all right?"

He came into the room and sat on the side of the bed. "You've been looking so pale and tired lately." He took her hand and rubbed it against his cheek. "I think we should move to San Francisco now. I want you near your doctor and the hospital. If anything happened to you—"

His voice broke and he bent down and took her

in his arms. Her traitorous heart was pounding madly at his touch. Would it never learn not to trust him?

She held him and stroked his head as she murmured, "I'm fine, just tired. This son of yours is a pretty big fellow for me to carry around all the time."

He sat up and unbuttoned her silk smock. "I'm going to put you to bed and I want you to stay there."

He undressed her with gentleness and helped her into her tentlike nightgown, then pulled the covers around her and kissed her good night.

When he was gone, she settled into the softness of the satin sheets and wished he had come to bed with her. She needed his closeness and his reassurance. In spite of the doctor's optimism, she was frightened. She didn't know what to expect. Would she have a long-drawn-out labor? The baby was so big—she hoped that the delivery would be easy and pose no danger. Shane would never forgive her if anything happened to his son.

She drifted off into sleep and woke an hour later feeling refreshed. The memory of Shane's tenderness brought a smile. He hadn't seemed to pay much attention to her lately and she was surprised that he'd noticed she wasn't feeling well.

She got out of bed and put on her robe and slippers. It was still early—she'd join Shane downstairs and reassure him that all she'd needed was a little rest. Her soft slippers on the thickly carpeted stairway were soundless. The haunting strains of a violin concerto floated from the stereo speakers and she turned at the bottom of the stairs, started into the living room, then stopped and stared. Shane was standing by the grand piano with his back to her holding Audrey in his arms! Audrey had her face buried in his shoulder but something attracted her attention and she looked up. Her turquoise eyes caught Karen's green ones and held them for a moment, then her arms tightened around Shane's neck and she once again snuggled into his shoulder. Karen whirled and fled back up the stairs!

The long night was finally over and when Karen opened her eyes the sun was high in the sky. At three o'clock she'd given up and taken a sleeping pill and slept till ten. Her head ached and she felt groggy and unable to cope with what she had seen last night. Shane and Audrey! Couldn't he have waited until the baby was born before bringing Audrey here as his mistress?

She dragged herself out of bed, dressed, and went downstairs to the dining room. The thought of food made her ill but she poured herself a cup of coffee before she became aware of voices coming from the small adjoining kitchen. She recognized them as Audrey's and Mrs. Whitney's. They were the last two people she wanted to see, but as she turned to leave she bumped into a chair and pushed it into the table with a scraping sound.

Audrey appeared in the doorway and there was a look of triumph on her face as she said, "Oh, Karen, I didn't know you were up." She made a little face. "Sorry you walked in on Shane and me at the wrong moment last night,

but if you're going to spy you'd better expect to
learn some unpleasant truths."

Anger pricked at Karen's shattered ego. "I
wasn't spying. Need I remind you that this is *my*
house and Shane is *my* husband. What's the
matter, Audrey, can't you find a man of your
own?"

Audrey bristled but her voice was sugary as
she said, "Oh, but Karen, Shane *is* my man.
Have you forgotten he only married you to give
him a child?"

Karen jerked to attention. How could Audrey
know that? Shane had been insistent that no one
but Mark should know the circumstances of
their marriage. Her surprise must have shown,
because Audrey laughed.

"I'm afraid Shane hasn't been entirely truthful. In fact, he couldn't face a scene with you
this morning so I agreed to take the brunt of your
hysterics. He left, poor baby. He hates crying
women. He'll be back when you're calmed
down."

She turned toward the coffee urn and poured
herself a cup of coffee. "I told him you were too
young and inexperienced to be involved in this
little plan of ours, but he felt sorry for you after
your house burned down and let his paternal
instincts get the better of his good sense. Now,
of course, he regrets his generous impulse, but
the baby will be born soon and you can go on
your way and Shane and I can be married."

Karen's knees gave way and she sank down on
a chair, stunned, unable to comprehend what
Audrey was saying. What did she mean Shane
hadn't been truthful? Why does she say *our* little

plan, as if she had been involved in it, too? If Shane and Audrey were in love why hadn't he married her in the first place?

Audrey sat down across the table from Karen and lit a cigarette as she continued, "I'm sorry—I guess I'm not making much sense to you. You know, of course, that Shane and I are lovers. We want to marry but he has this thing about needing a son to carry on the family business and I—"her voice broke but Karen saw the calculating expression in her eyes—"I was in an accident a few years ago and can never have children."

The words were coming through loud and clear, and Karen couldn't shut them out as Audrey went on. "Actually, it was my idea to pay someone to have his child and give it to him. I didn't see any reason for him to marry the mother, but he wanted the child to be legitimate, so I went along with it. He put the ad in the paper and came up with you."

Karen squirmed in her chair, trying to get away from the hateful, cutting words, but each one found its mark with true precision. Audrey continued to aim them well.

"It was a nuisance when Mark fell in love with you and insisted on protecting your rights with that premarital contract. It made for a lot of haggling that could have been avoided. Both Shane and I knew you had such a crush on Shane that you would give him anything he wanted, even custody of his son as soon as it was born, but Mark interfered and made him agree to let you keep the child for eight years."

She grinned an evil little grin and smirked.

"You realize, of course, that the agreement is not legal and Shane has no intention of letting you keep the child? He'll divorce you, but *we'll* keep the baby."

Rage combined with a touch of hysteria set off fireworks in Karen as she jumped to her feet and shouted, "The devil you will! You're not raising my child! I think you're making all this up because you're jealous!"

"Jealous! Of you?" Audrey laughed and got to her feet, stubbing the cigarette out in the ash tray. "Don't be silly—why should I be jealous of you? All you're going to get out of Shane is a child he won't even let you see and a lot of money. Well, I already have plenty of money, and I'll get the child whether I want it or not. Oh, no, Karen, I'm not jealous of you. If you want the truth, I feel sorry for you."

She turned and walked out of the room.

Karen stood there gaping, turmoil boiling up inside her. Shane had been lying to her all along, playing with her emotions. He'd planned the whole thing with Audrey! His concern for her future, his offer to annul the marriage and send her to school, his unwillingness to take advantage of her innocence—all were part of an act, a means of getting what he wanted from her: a son. He had deliberately used his experience and expertise to inflame her passion and her love. That was the cruelest cut of all. He'd made her fall in love with him, hoping she'd hand over the baby without protest when it was born, and she'd been naive enough to mistake his unbridled lust for the one thing she wanted most—his love. He had no intention of letting her raise her child—not even for eight years. He would marry Audrey and turn their son over to *her* to raise!

Before Karen could pull herself together and act, Mrs. Whitney came into the room—Mrs. Whitney, in her inevitable dark dress and the sleek heavy chignon at the back of her long slender neck. Karen had never seen her with a wrinkle in her clothes or a hair out of place. She was the perfect housekeeper and her dislike for Karen was so intense that it pulsated through the room when they were alone together as they were now. She said nothing—she never spoke to Karen with disrespect—but her eyes before she turned away were filled with scorn and— ridicule? Karen knew Mrs. Whitney had been listening to Audrey's tirade.

As though a spring had been released in her Karen rushed out of the room and up the stairs. She would never allow Audrey to raise her child! She'd leave, get as far away as she could, someplace where Shane would never find her.

She pulled two suitcases from her closet and packed one with maternity clothes, then took the other one down the hall to the room they had fixed up as a temporary nursery. She paused in the doorway, her eyes blinded by unshed tears. She'd been so touched when Shane had insisted they decorate one of the rooms as a nursery, even though they'd known she and the baby would be there only a short time. He'd even gone with her to pick out baby furniture and had taken such pride in the solid maple Early American-style crib and chest.

The cheat! He'd known all along the baby would be there long after she left! She squared her shoulders and started packing tiny garments. She'd have to hurry. It was vital that she leave before Shane came back and stopped her, but first she had to write a note. She couldn't just walk out and take the chance that he might think she'd been kidnapped, as had happened when his mother left.

Back in her room she sat at her desk and scribbled hastily:

Shane,
  Audrey told me everything. After what I saw last night I have no choice but to believe her. I'll never let her raise my child so I'm going away. Please don't try to find me. I'll take good care of the baby. I promise.
  I really did love you so much!

She signed it and pinned it to his pillow so he would be sure to find it, then put on her all-weather coat and carried her cases to the top of the stairs.

All was quiet. She lugged the heavy suitcases down the steps and paused; the exertion had caused a painful stitch in her side. There was no one around as she hurried out the door and around to the garage.

Audrey's Ferrari was gone and so was Shane's Cadillac. She breathed a little easier as she put her bags in the trunk of the small compact car that Mrs. Whitney usually drove shopping. It was several years old and a light tan; it looked like thousands of other cars on the California highways.

There were several car keys on her key ring and it took three trys before the engine turned over and she eased the car out of the garage, down the driveway, and onto Seventeen Mile Drive. If she could just get out of Carmel without running into Shane or Audrey. But first she had to stop at the bank.

The late-afternoon rush-hour traffic was the worst Karen had ever experienced and the closer she came to Los Angeles the worse it got. She was tired to the point of exhaustion; her head throbbed and her nerves were shot. It seemed as if she had been strapped into the bucket seat forever. She hadn't stopped the car since she had headed it out of Carmel toward Highway 101 and turned south. That was hours ago and she still had no destination. Her only thought was to put as much distance between herself and Shane as she could before he discovered that she was gone and came after her.

A blaring horn and the screech of brakes jerked Karen's attention back to the road, and she realized that she'd inadvertently crossed the white line into the next lane. That did it! It was time to stop before she caused an accident. Besides, she knew Shane would have the highway patrol looking for her when he realized she wasn't coming back.

An overhead sign above the freeway indicated that the next several turnoffs were to Santa Barbara. Karen began to maneuver the car into the right hand lane so she could take one of the exits. She was only vaguely familiar with Santa Barbara. She'd been there a few times with her parents years ago and remembered being impressed by the palm trees and the Spanish-style architecture of the oceanside city, but now it was a jumble of streets that took off in different directions and the traffic made her want to scream with frustration. A lighted sign on the motel up ahead said VACANCY and she turned into the driveway. Right now all she wanted was a bed on which she could lie down and go to sleep.

Morning brought a new day, the second day of Karen's flight. Where was she going and what would she do when she got there? These and other questions ran through her mind as she lay quietly, watching the sun stream through the window and listening to the steady hum of traffic outside her room. She felt disillusioned, bewildered, and lonely. How could she support a child when she couldn't even support herself?

She had five thousand dollars with her—all the money that had been in the bank account Shane had opened for her. It wouldn't keep her for very long, not with hospital expenses to pay. She glanced down at the rings on her hands. Her engagement and wedding bands. Delicate strands of gold set with diamonds. They must be worth a small fortune. A tremor ran through her as she hastily shoved her hands under the covers. In an emergency she could pawn her rings, but it would break her heart. In the meantime, she'd find a small apartment; she couldn't afford twenty dollars a day for a motel room.

Maybe she'd just stay here in Santa Barbara.

The climate was ideal and Shane would have no reason to look for her here. She shuddered. It wouldn't be easy to hide from Shane! She remembered the unbelievable lengths he'd gone to, to have her investigated before choosing her as the mother of his child. He would be even more ruthless now that she was hiding his baby from him.

If only she weren't so alone! If only there were someone she could turn to, but she couldn't contact anyone she'd ever known. Shane would find them and through them he'd find her and her child. He'd take her baby away from her!

She tossed uncomfortably. She ached in every muscle, probably from sitting in one position on the long drive yesterday. She struggled out of bed and went to the bathroom, brushed her teeth, and took a warm, pulsating shower. It didn't help much and she crawled back into bed with a sigh. She should get dressed and go out for breakfast, buy a paper and start looking for an apartment, but she just didn't feel up to it. Maybe after another hour or two of sleep . . .

When she woke again it was eleven o'clock and the ache had settled in her lower back. She shifted position, but it didn't help. She got up and dressed and went in search of a coffee shop. There was one just a few doors down from her motel, and as she picked up the menu she remembered that she hadn't eaten at all yesterday. She shivered. She didn't want to think of yesterday.

The omelette she'd ordered was good but she could hardly sit still. She shifted position as she stood waiting to pay her bill and the woman behind the cashier's counter looked at her with open sympathy and said, "Got much longer to go?"

Karen shook her head. "Only about a month, but it seems like forever."

She paid for her meal and bought a paper, but by the time she got back to her room her stomach was upset and she didn't seem to be able to sit or stand in any position that relieved the pain in her back. She undressed again and went back to bed. Driving so far yesterday must have exhausted her even more than she'd realized—maybe she'd better just rest today and not try to do anything until tomorrow.

She dozed but couldn't get away from the back pain. Maybe if she got up and took an aspirin it would help, but her stomach was so upset that she was afraid to try to swallow anything.

She slept, but woke just in time to make a mad dash for the bathroom, where she was violently ill. She was leaning against the shower stall, fighting the weakness that made the room spin, when a swift, hot thrust of pain in the lower part of her abdomen caused her to cry out and double up, her face contorted in agony.

Realization came and she made her way shakily to the bedside table and picked up the telephone. When the operator answered she said, "This is Karen McKittrick in Room Five. Call a taxi, please, I think I'm about to have my baby!"

What happened after that was a blur. There were waves of pain and people in her room, then the ride in an ambulance with sirens screaming and the hospital emergency room.

Finally, before they could even transfer her to

the delivery room, the pain built to a crescendo and she remembered screaming for Shane, then the pain stopped and she heard the shrill cry of an infant. The doctor's smiling face beamed down at her from above and said, "You have a six-and-a-half-pound daughter, Karen, and she seems strong and healthy."

Karen never had a chance to reply as she sank into soft black weightlessness.

The hall outside the nursery was deserted except for an occasional nurse, who walked by on crepe-soled shoes, and Karen, dressed in a flowing pink robe and matching slippers. She stood with her forehead pressed against the window that separated her from the incubator housing her small daughter. Her heart swelled with love as she watched the energetic baby suck on her fist. She was hungry and they would soon bring her to Karen to be nursed.

She shifted her position and rubbed her hand over her flat stomach. She had a waist again and it seemed so good to be able to bend over and put her slippers on. It was great to feel like a woman instead of a baby factory—and that was all she had ever been to Shane.

Karen sighed as her attention once more shifted to the baby. She looked so much like Shane. Her hair and eyes were dark and even at four days she had the same stubborn set of the jaw as her father. Her father. Karen hunched her shoulders against the anguish the thought of Shane still caused her. It was her own fault. Why did she have to be so stupid? He'd lied to her, cheated her, planned to take her baby away from her, and still she longed for him with an ache that was almost unbearable. She should hate him, but every night she dreamed of his lips on hers, his hands caressing her, his body responding to her with an urgent need, until she woke with tears streaming down her cheeks.

She knew she was doomed to a lifetime of pain because every time she looked at his daughter she would see him. He would have been proud of Shanna—or would he? He had wanted a son—he had made that quite clear. Maybe he wouldn't have wanted this baby after all. She grimaced. That was a premise she couldn't count on. Shane would lodge a full-scale search for her; she'd have to get further away. As soon as she and the baby were stronger they'd go east. Texas, maybe. It wouldn't be easy for him to find her in Texas.

But first she had to get out of the hospital. She was due to be dismissed tomorrow. Mrs. Waverly, the hospital's social worker, had found her a small apartment. Karen had asked for help but told Mrs. Waverly only that she and her husband were separated and that he would not be supporting her. She'd asked that the birth not be publicized and said that under no circumstances were they to contact her husband. She was paying the bill so they were content to allow her to call the shots, but she'd have to leave Santa Barbara soon. She'd given her own name and address to the hospital and she knew it wouldn't take Shane long to find her.

Karen shifted her position again and knew she'd have to return to her room to lie down. Standing still for too long tired her. She whispered "goodbye" through the glass to her daughter and started down the hall. There was a man coming toward her from the opposite end of the long passageway. At first she didn't really notice him but then something made her look again. It was Shane! For just a moment her emotions overruled her good sense and a powerful surge of joy flooded over her. She wanted to run to him, throw herself in his arms, hold him. Then she remembered. He wasn't coming for her—he was going to take her baby!

By this time Shane was sprinting down the hall, closing the gap between them. Karen turned and ran back toward the nursery. She had to protect her child! She'd fight with every bit of her strength to keep him away from her daughter!

Unfortunately, what little strength she had was used up before she'd gone more than a few steps and the walls began to spin as the pounding in her ears became a roar, and if it hadn't been for the strong arms that picked her up and held her against the familiar chest she would have fallen.

As Shane carried her down the corridor she pounded him with her fists and screamed, "No! No! I won't let you take my baby! You can't have her! She's mine!"

Shane must have known which room was hers because he quickly turned into it as two nurses ran toward them, attracted by Karen's frantic behavior. They were both yelling at Shane and he turned and glared at them as he said, "I'm Shane McKittrick and Karen is my wife. I'm not going to hurt her; I just want to talk to her. Now if you will please leave I promise we'll call you if we need you."

They looked at Karen, who by this time was

completely exhausted and lay quietly in Shane's arms. He looked grim but when he spoke again it was a soft appeal.

"Please. We've had a misunderstanding that has to be straightened out. We need a few minutes alone to talk."

The well-known McKittrick charm worked and the nurses smiled as they turned and walked out of the room, shutting the door behind them.

Shane sat down in the big armchair and cradled her on his lap. She knew she was beaten. She's used up all her reserves and she couldn't fight him anymore. Her tears came in great wrenching sobs as he rocked her back and forth in his arms. His lips caressed her hair and he was murmuring something to her but she couldn't hear above her wailing.

She was curled up on his lap crying as if her heart would break and his voice was torn with emotion as he said, "Karen, darling, don't cry so hard. You're killing me by inches, do you know that?"

Karen swallowed a sob and looked up at him through pools of tears. He'd aged in the week since she'd last seen him. But how was that possible? He looked older, tired, his face gray and lined. His hair, always immaculately styled, was disheveled and the torment in his eyes matched the torment she saw in her own whenever she looked in a mirror. He'd suffered as much as she had. She'd known he'd be enraged over her leaving but she hadn't realized that he'd be this concerned about the baby. Any hope she'd had that he might relent and let her raise the child was dashed. He obviously didn't trust her to care for it properly or he wouldn't have suffered so when he thought she'd taken it from him. Well, this was one time she wasn't going to give in to him.

She buried her face in his shoulder and shuddered as she said, "Shane, I'll fight you with every weapon I can find. I'll be a good mother; I'll never allow Audrey to raise my daughter."

He stroked her hair. "Of course you won't. Neither would I. Nobody's going to raise our daughter but her parents—you and me, Karen."

She raised her head, startled. "But Audrey said—"

Shane's face hardened. "I know what Audrey said and I probably would have killed her for it if I hadn't been so desperate to find you."

"What!" Karen shrieked.

He pulled her close and guided her head back to his shoulder. "I'd gone into Carmel on business that morning and when I got home and found your note I went nearly out of my mind. I didn't know what you were talking about but I knew Audrey must have said something awful to drive you away like that and I went looking for her." He shivered. "It will be a cold day in hell before she forgets that encounter! I didn't take long to get the truth out of her and when she finished telling me . . ."

Karen sat up again, her eyes wide. "Shane?"

The look on his face softened and he rubbed the tears from her eyes with his thumb. "My precious darling, don't you know even yet how much I love you?"

She gasped. "L-love me?"

"Adore you, worship you. There isn't a word strong enough for the way I feel about you,

Karen. I've loved you ever since I first saw you but I've fought it every step of the way. I was Shane McKittrick, the invincible. No woman was ever going to mean anything to me. I would never be hurt by a woman the way my father was!"

For the first time he smiled. "Then you came along and walked right into my heart and I didn't have a chance. I tried every way I knew to dislodge you. I stayed away from you, spent most of my time in San Francisco, and missed you so much I couldn't stand it. I tried to send you away and wound up in the hospital with a broken head and a need for you that was frightening. I moved you out of my bed and then paced the floor in agony every night."

His voice broke and he gathered her to him as his seeking mouth covered hers. Karen was lightheaded with joy and confusion. Had he really said he loved her? He'd never said that before—ever. His actions often told her that his feelings for her were deeper than he would admit, but he'd never told her that he loved her—not even in their most intimate moments.

She wound her arms around his neck and held him as their kiss plumbed the depth of their love. Shane groaned and buried his face in the soft hollow of her neck beneath her ear as he whispered, "Don't ever leave me again, little one! Don't even go shopping or for a walk without telling me where you're going and when you'll be back. I couldn't survive another week like this one. Hell would have been a vacation compared to what I've been through!"

She held his head against her and stroked her fingers through his hair as she murmured, "I'm sorry, darling, but Audrey was so convincing, and Shane, I did see her in your arms that night."

Shane shuddered and held her tighter. "Oh, Karen, if you'd only come in that room a minute earlier or a minute later none of this would have happened. I wasn't making love to Audrey; she tripped and started to fall and I caught her. You must have come in during the second or so it took to steady her. If you'd only said something—shouted at me, anything—I could have explained. As it was, I didn't even know you'd been there until I forced it out of Audrey."

Karen winced. "She said you wanted to marry her but that she couldn't have children—that it was her idea to advertise for a woman to give you a child."

Shane took her face in his hands and looked deep into her green eyes. "Karen, I swear to you I never had any intention of marrying Audrey. I never intended to marry anyone until you came along and started tormenting me without even meaning to. Audrey was simply a diversion, as many other women have been. I'm thirty-two years old, sweetheart, and I'm not a monk."

"What I told you about the newspaper ad was true. Mark and I were the only ones who knew about it. Audrey learned about it from Mrs. Whitney, who had been listening at keyholes and told her."

"Mrs. Whitney!" Karen screeched in disbelief. "But she's always been the perfect housekeeper! Why would she do a thing like that?"

Shane's mouth twisted with disgust. "Because Audrey was paying her to discourage beautiful women from taking an interest in me. Audrey had apparently decided that she wanted to be Mrs. Shane McKittrick, and what Audrey wants Audrey usually gets. I finally found out that's why Mrs. Whitney put you in the servants' quarters when you first came. She knew she'd better keep you out of my way if she didn't want me distracted. Then I found out about it and threatened to fire her and she's hated you ever since. She was only too happy to take revenge that way."

Karen shivered. "How awful!"

Shane shrugged. "I had to restrain myself to keep from throwing her out bodily. I gave her an hour to pack and leave and told her that if she made any more trouble I'd see to it that she never worked anywhere again. As for Audrey, someone said she's gone to Europe." His voice was grim. "If she's smart she'll stay there!"

Without warning the door opened and a nurse appeared with a small pink bundle in her arms. She grinned and said, "I have a little one here who's been screaming for her dinner. You'd better help her, Mama, before Miss McKittrick starves to death."

Karen wiggled off Shane's lap and took off her robe, then climbed onto the bed. The nurse raised it to a sitting position and handed Karen the fussing bundle. The nurse left and Karen motioned Shane to sit on the side of the bed. His eyes took in all the details of the dark-haired little girl and Karen smiled as she said, "What do you think of your daughter?"

He put out a finger and touched her almost reverently. "Does she have a name?"

"Of course," Karen answered. "Since we were going to call the baby Shane Alexander, Jr., if it was a boy, I named her Shanna Alexandria. It was the closest I could get."

Shane said nothing but continued to watch the nursing child. His expression was unreadable and Karen felt uneasy. There was one question she had to ask.

"Shane, are you terribly disappointed that she wasn't a boy?"

Shane looked up, surprised. "Why on earth should I be disappointed. She's a beautiful baby. Someday she may be almost as special as her mother." He took Karen's hand and kissed it, then held it to his cheek.

Her fingers caressed his face as she murmured, "But you wanted a son—an heir, to carry on the business."

He grinned. "Mrs. McKittrick, what makes you think a woman can't head a business just as efficiently as a man?"

Karen laughed and leaned over to kiss him, unwittingly dislodging the baby's dinner. Shanna screamed in protest and Shane rolled his eyes heavenward in mock horror.

"My stars, woman, quit messing around and feed the poor child! It's easy to see that she has an appetite like her mother's."

When Shanna was finally satisfied and fell asleep, the nurse came and carried her back to her crib. Shane adjusted the bed so Karen was lying flat, then took off his shoes and lay down beside her. He took her in his arms and held her full-length against him as he said, "We got in all kinds of trouble in the hospital in Santa Cruz for lying on the bed together, but I can't be in the same room with you and not hold you."

His lips caressed her face and when he spoke

again there was a throb in his voice. "Can you ever forgive me for driving you away, making you go through the experience of giving birth to our child alone before I would admit that I love you and want you with me always? I've been such a blind, self-centered fool! I went through hell to protect myself from something I know now would never have happened. I wouldn't grow up and admit that my mother was the exception, not the rule."

He drew her closer and his lips trailed kisses down the side of her neck as he murmured, "Oh, Karen, I love you so!"

She snuggled against him and stroked his nape and back, letting her body tell him of her love. He kissed her gently but with a suppressed hunger and said, "I told you once that I wasn't sure I could live without you. Well, my darling, now I know for sure that I can't. Karen, will you come home with me and be my wife, for as long as we both shall live?"

Karen could only nod, her throat too choked with emotion to speak. But she knew Shane could see the joy shining from her face. Those were the words she'd waited so long to hear! She turned to him, her eyes glowing with the love they shared.

ROMANCE THE WAY
IT USED TO BE...
AND COULD BE AGAIN

Contemporary romances for today's women

*Each month, six very special love stories will
be yours from SILHOUETTE. Look for them
wherever books are sold or order now
from the coupon below.*

_____#16 SECOND TOMORROW Anne Hampson
$1.50 (57016-1)

_____#17 TORMENTING FLAME Nancy John
$1.50 (57017-X)

_____#18 THE LION'S SHADOW Elizabeth Hunter
$1.50 (57018-8)

_____#19 THE HEART NEVER FORGETS Carolyn Thornton
$1.50 (57019-6)

_____#20 ISLAND DESTINY Paula Fulford
$1.50 (57020-X)

_____#21 SPRING FIRES Leigh Richards $1.50 (57021-8)

_____#22 MEXICAN NIGHTS Jeanne Stephens
$1.50 (57022-6)

_____#23 BEWITCHING GRACE Paula Edwards
$1.50 (57023-4)

_____#24 SUMMER STORM Letitia Healy $1.50 (57024-2)

_____#25 SHADOW OF LOVE Sondra Stanford
$1.50 (57025-0)

_____#26 INNOCENT FIRE Brooke Hastings
$1.50 (57026-9)

_____#27 THE DAWN STEALS SOFTLY Anne Hampson
$1.50 (57027-7)

_____#28 MAN OF THE OUTBACK Anne Hampson
$1.50 (57028-5)

_____#29 RAIN LADY Faye Wildman $1.50 (57029-3)

_____#30 RETURN ENGAGEMENT Diana Dixon
$1.50 (57030-7)

_____#31 TEMPORARY BRIDE Phyllis Halldorson
$1.50 (57031-5)

_____#32 GOLDEN LASSO Fern Michaels $1.50 (57032-3)

_____#33 A DIFFERENT DREAM Donna Vitek
$1.50 (57033-1)